The Lady and the Lollards

Ray Filby

The Lady and the Lollards

Publisher : Midhurst

Published by Midhurst

Copyright © Ray Filby 2020

This is a work of fiction.
Apart from obvious historic personages,
any resemblance to actual persons,
living or dead, is purely coincidental.

Midhurst.
2, Freers Mews,
Warwick,
Warwickshire,
CV34 6DP

ISBN 978-1-8380437-4-2

http://midhurstpublishing.uk

Acknowledgements

The author would like to thank his wife, Sue, for proof reading, for her constructive suggestions and for her patience and encouragement during the writing of this story.

8

Contents

Introduction	11
List of Characters featured in story	13
Chapter 1 The Lady	19
Chapter 2 The King	23
Chapter 3 The Queen	31
Chapter 4 The Maid	39
Chapter 5 The Duke	45
Chapter 6 The Battle of Towton	55
Chapter 7 The Lollards	63
Chapter 8 Helmsley Castle	73
Chapter 9 Pickering Castle	81
Chapter 10 The Escape	93
Chapter 11 The Orphanage	109
Chapter 12 The Turncoats	121
Chapter 13 Enemies Reconciled	129
Chapter 14 The Tower	135
Chapter 15 The Rescue	153
Chapter 16 Rewards and Punishments	169

Appendices

Line of descent of House of Lancaster   183

Line of descent of House of York   185

Battles fought during the Hundred Years' War   187

Battles fought during the War of the Roses   191

List of Old Etonian Prime Ministers   193

Prominent Alumni of King's College, Cambridge University   195

Prominent Female Alumni of Queens' College, Cambridge University   197

Books published by Midhurst   199

Introduction

The story is set in the reign of Henry VI, the most tumultuous reign in English history, coming at the end of the Hundred Years' War and covering most of the War of the Roses. The author therefore hopes the reader will bear with him as he includes a significant amount of historic detail in the early part of the book which is necessary to provide the context in which the main story is set.

Because of the complexity of the historic and dynastic setting, tables have been provided as appendices giving the outline family trees of the Houses of Lancaster and York, and a list of the main battles fought in the wars within which the story is set. To avoid confusion in identifying the characters in the book, a list is included at the beginning of the book, providing a who's who of the main characters featuring in the story. This was felt to be specially necessary as a fairly limited number of forenames seem to be in use during that period of history, leading to duplication.

The story is of course a work of fiction but the author has tried to remain faithful to the known historic events of the time. In some cases, there have been contradictions in the sources used but a television presenter as eminent as the historian, Dr. Lucy Worsley, has declared that much of the history we receive in text books provides a distorted presentation of the facts and is coloured by the interests of the people who write history for posterity. The author doesn't therefore feel bad that there will be inaccuracies and distortions of history found in his own work of fiction. While I wouldn't recommend historic fiction as a vehicle for learning history, it at least helps to cement the knowledge derived from a study of more authentic sources of history.

Characters featured in this story

As the story covers a lengthy period of history, many names come up. While most of these are important in their historic setting, they do not necessarily play an important role in the development of this story. Also, many names crop up more than once, e.g. Henry, Edward and Richard. There are even two 'Henry Beauforts' two Edwards, Princes of Wales!.

Therefore, to assist the reader to keep track of the characters, two list have been provided. One list defines the status of the main characters in the story. The other list, printed in smaller type, gives the names of the other personages who may be important in their own right but who are no more than minor characters, whose names may appear once or twice only in the story.

Main Characters

Constance	the Lady
Matthew	the Lollards
Michael	

King Henry VI	Henry of Windsor
Queen Margaret of Anjou	
Edward	Prince of Wales (1)

Council of regency during King Henry's minority

Humphrey, Duke of Gloucester   King's uncles
John, Duke of Bedford
Cardinal Henry Beaufort   Bishop of Winchester

William de la Pole, Earl of Suffolk
      Ambassador to France and Queen's favourite

Henry Beaufort, Duke of Somerset
         Commander of Lancastrian army

Baron Thomas de Ros   Chatelains of Helmsley
Baroness Philippa de Ros   Castle

Joan of Arc   Maid of Orleans
Pierre Cauchon   Bishop of Beauvais

King Edward IV   son of Richard of York
Queen Elizabeth   Elizabeth Woodville
Edward   Prince of Wales (2), later
                        became King Edward V
Richard, Duke of York   father of Edward IV

Baron John Howard   later became Duke
                          of Norfolk
Giles Noirmont   Black Giles

Richard Neville, Earl of   Kingmaker who
    Warwick   changed sides

Alice Chaucer, Duchess of Suffolk

Minor Characters

Prominent Lancastrians

Duke of Exeter   Earl of Northumberland
Lord Ralph Dacre   Earl of Devon
Earl of Wiltshire

Prominent Yorkists

Earl of Salisbury   Lord Fauconburg, Earl of Kent

French Royalty and Personages

Charles VI (Charles the mad)
Catherine of Valois   daughter of Charles VI and
                               mother of Henry VI
Charles VII (Charles the Victorious)   son of Charles VI
Louis XI (Louis the Prudent)   son of Charles VII

Rene, Duke of Anjou   father of Queen Margaret
Isabella of Lorraine   mother of Queen Margaret

Scottish Royalty

James II
Margaret of Gueldes   wife of James II, friend of
                               Queen Margaret

James III

Historical Predecessors

Henry V   Henry VI's father and victor
                               at Agincourt
Henry IV   Henry VI's grandfather
John of Gaunt (Ghent)   Duke of Lancaster
                             Henry VI's great grandfather

Richard II	King deposed by Henry IV
William of Wykeham	Cardinal Beaufort's predecessor as Bishop of Winchester

Domestic Servants and Country Folk

Robin Standing	Chief Cook at Pickering Castle
Alice	Kitchen maid at Pickering Castle
Jacob	Orphan of Helmsley
Joseph	Steward of Helmsley Castle
James	Spokesman for Helmsley farmers
Agnes	Kitchen maid at Tower of London

Holders of Religious Offices

Prebendary Richard Hayman	Vicar of St. Peter's, Ulleskelf
Reverend Will Hakford	Vicar of All Saints, Helmsley
Thomas Bouchier	Archbishop of Canterbury
George Nevill	Archbishop of York
Lawrence Booth	Archbishop of York
William Martyn	Abbott of Waverley Abbey

Holders of Civilian Office

Edmund de Ros	Chatelain of Helmsley Castle Son of Thomas and Philippa
John Sutton, Baron Dudley	Constable of the Tower of London
Sir Richard Tempest	Owner of Weddington Hall place where King Henry sought refuge

Other Royal Personages

George, Duke of Clarence	brother of King Edward IV
Isabel, Duchess of Clarence	George's wife and daughter of the Earl of Warwick

Richard, Duke of Gloucester   brother of King Edward IV
Anne, Duchess of Gloucester   Richard's wife and daughter of
                                            the Earl of Warwick
            later to become King Richard III and Queen Anne

Henry Tudor, Earl of Richmond,
                          later to become King Henry VII

Reformers

John Wycliffe, Vicar of Lutterworth
                        founder of the Lollard movement
John Huss   Bohemian Reformer
Huldrych Zwingli   Swiss Reformer
John Calvin   French Reformer
Martin Luther   German Reformer

Chapter 1

The Lady

Lady Constance had decided that the last thing she wanted was a relationship with a knight. She felt irritated by the fact that Oliver de Barton, one of the complement of knights which garrisoned Helmsley Castle, had blown her a kiss as he swaggered across the great hall where she was sitting in an alcove, engaged in her embroidery. Constance was a very beautiful girl in her late teens. She looked particularly attractive today in a long green dress, her neatly braided hair carefully arranged under a wimple. Her company was much sought after at Helmsley, but Constance found the knights to be arrogant, conceited and boastful young men and she wasn't swayed by the fact that many of them were strong and handsome. Their conversation seemed to be limited to the feats of arms they had achieved, the exaggerated claims to the numbers they had slain on the battlefield and their precedence in the household. Their turn of phrase and language was coarse, so that they unwittingly came over to Constance as ignorant young men.

In reality, Constance was not a titled noble woman, but was always referred to as Lady Constance since she had effectively become the adopted daughter of Baron and Baroness Thomas and Philippa de Ros, the chatelains of Helmsley Castle. Constance's parents had been tenants on the estate belonging to Baron Thomas de Ros. The Baron did not regard those who worked on his estate as feudal vassals with few personal rights and owing him full personal allegiance as their overlord. He arranged for his estate to be subdivided into farms and smallholdings, run by tenant farmers with a contingent of farm workers. The farms were productive and the rents were very reasonable. Baron Thomas de Ros was well known and popular among those who farmed on his land. They were more loyal to him than the workers on the estates of other landed gentry where the feudal system still operated in much the way it had done in the days of William the Conqueror.

Constance's mother had died when she was eleven and her father had been killed when he tried to prevent Baron de Ros's cattle from being rustled by soldiers serving Baron John Howard, the owner of another local estate. Baron Thomas de Ros naturally made the strongest possible protest to Baron Howard at this highhanded act of theft of his property but was met with scorn and derision from Baron John Howard.

"If you were stupid enough to fight on the side of our pathetic king at the battle of St. Albans, you deserve to lose your possessions. The Duke of York holds sway now and he'll favour me over you should you approach him to regain your wretched cattle."

John Howard spoke with a contemptuous snarl. Thomas de Ros knew what he said was true. John Howard had sided with York's victorious rebel army at St. Albans. No chance of Thomas de Ros getting restoration of his possessions by going through official channels and he didn't have the resources to enter into conflict with John Howard with any hope of achieving successful outcome with the return of the stolen cattle. However, Thomas de Ros didn't expect this state of affairs to be permanent. He'd just have to wait his chance and take it when the tide turned.

In view of her father's faithful service and the fact that he had died, protecting their property, Lord and Lady de Ros felt in honour bound to take Constance into the protection of their household.

They soon realised that this had been very beneficial to themselves for besides being beautiful, Constance was capable, intelligent and dutiful. She proved to be of inestimable benefit to Philippa de Ros in running the household at Helmsley Castle.

Lady Philippa had a social conscience and was frequently seen in her neighbourhood, distributing alms to tenants she knew were in difficulty or visiting the sick. She was always glad to have Constance with her as she made these sorties from the castle. Constance was well known and liked, both by the people of Helmsley and the neighbouring villages. Among the tasks in which Constance had been involved were providing comfort to families which had been recently bereaved, assisting a midwife to deliver a child on two occasions, and providing domestic service to a family at a time when the housewife was unwell and unfit for work.

What had caused England to descend into the near anarchy it was now experiencing? We'll need to go back a few years to understand the historic context of the situation which now existed. This was in no small way due to the vulnerable state of the monarchy at the time..

Chapter 2

The King

Henry had been proclaimed king at the tender age of nine months after the premature death of his father, the renowned King Henry V, victor at Agincourt. After this victory, a settlement known as the Treaty of Troyes was made. By this treaty, the new young king, often referred to as Henry of Windsor by virtue of his birthplace, had a claim to the French throne on the death of the current king of France, Charles VI. This claim came through his mother, Catherine of Valois, daughter of the French king and wife of Henry V. During the minority of young Henry, England was governed by a team who acted as regents, his uncles, John, Dule of Bedford, and Humphrey, Duke of Gloucester, and his great uncle, Cardinal Henry Beaufort, Bishop of Winchester. These three, who formed the Council of Regency, were discussing the situation in France.

"Things have started to go badly in France," began Humphrey of Gloucester, a somewhat pompous middle-aged aristocrat. "A new phenomenon has emerged in France. A female leader has come to the fore and she's inspiring the French armies to the success which has hitherto eluded them. Her name is Joan. She's not of noble birth but was born of peasant stock in a village called Arc, can you believe it. She claims to be divinely inspired. In desperation, the Dauphin has allowed her to lead a French army."

"I know," responded his younger brother, John of Bedford. There was despondence in his voice. "She's raised the siege of Orleans which John Talbot, Earl of Shrewsbury, had surrounded. John didn't have sufficient forces take Orleans and by attacking his rear guard, Joan forced our troops into retreat. It seems that she harried our troops as they retreated to the Loire valley. A unit of archers which had been set up to block the pursuing French at Patay hadn't been properly prepared. It was scattered by the French cavalry who went on to inflict a major defeat on our troops. We lost over two-thousand men and they captured John Talbot!"

The trio sat in gloomy silence as they contemplated these unexpected reverses.

Cardinal Beaufort restarted the conversation.

"The worst news of all is that these French successes have emboldened the Dauphin to have himself proclaimed king and I gather he's proceeding to Reims for his coronation. This is a distinct violation of the Treaty of Troyes by which it was agreed that Henry should succeed to the French throne after the death of Charles VI. Indeed, Henry has already been proclaimed as king in France."

John Bedford commented, "The Dauphin has never accepted the validity of the Treaty of Troyes. He claims, that a king is not free to nominate his successor but is bound by the law of agnatic primogeniture. By this law, as it applies in France, the succession cannot proceed to a female or through a female line and Henry's claim is principally based on the fact that his mother, Catherine of Valois, is Charles VI's daughter and the Dauphin's sister. The Dauphin further claims that his father was known to be mad and therefore of diminished responsibility, not fit to sign the Treaty of Troyes with its implication for the future of the French monarchy."

The three again remained in subdued silence, none of them immediately having any idea of the course of action to be followed.
Humphrey Gloucester finally broke the silence.

"If the Dauphin Charles is getting himself crowned King of France, we must arrange a counter coronation for Henry."

"But he's only eight years old!" exclaimed John Bedford.

Humphrey continued, "That's old enough to sit through a coronation service and wear a crown!"

Henry Beaufort added a further appraisal of the young king.

"Henry really is a lovely kid. He's gentle, kind and considerate and in some areas, he has a maturity well beyond his years. He can read fluently and has a love of music and art. In particular he appreciates architecture. When we go to London to worship at Westminster Abbey or St. Paul's Cathedral, he sits in wonderment at the beauty of the gothic arcades and lofty vaulting. He particularly enjoys coming with me to Winchester where the nave, built in the time of my predecessor as bishop, William of Wykeham, is constructed in a particularly advanced evolution of gothic architecture.

The way he regards his immediate forebears is unusual. He shows no great excitement or pride in the great military feats of his father, Henry V, culminating in the spectacular victory at Agincourt where his small dispirited army, short of supplies, rallied to defeat the huge French army led by its heavy cavalry of knights and nobles. He is revolted by the suggestion that Henry possibly ordered the execution of some of the prisoners of war when it appeared they could have been rescued to turn the tide of battle. He strongly disapproves of the fact that his grandfather deposed King Richard in order to secure the throne for himself. The ancestor he really seems to admire is John of Gaunt (Ghent), Duke of Lancaster, who was a great supporter of my predecessor, William of Wykeham, and encouraged him in his founding of the school in Winchester and the New College at Oxford University. John of Gaunt also supported John Wycliffe and encouraged him in the promotion of his religious ideas, particularly commending him on his translation of the Bible into English. Henry has a copy of this translation and reads this avidly. He frequently expresses a wish that everyone should be taught to read so that they may receive the Word of God from Wycliffe's Bible as if God was speaking directly to them. He claims that although he's listened to many, many sermons, it wasn't until he read Wycliffe's Bible that he understood that salvation was by grace and not by works. That doesn't say much for my preaching," he added with a chuckle.

Humphrey Gloucester was not so enthusiastic in the declaration of the young king's merits.

"Yes, that's all very well and would be commendable if we lived in a world at peace but we don't. Now, it's very much a case of might is right and possessions must be fought for and won by force of arms. Sadly, Henry shows little enthusiasm during his lessons on swordsmanship and doesn't enjoy watching jousting. I fear that he'll never become a great war lord like his illustrious father and that's what'll be needed to maintain our control of France and curb the lawlessness which is now abroad in England at present. Still, that's besides the point. We must go ahead and arrange his coronation."

A few months after the Dauphin had himself crowned King Charles VII of France in Reims, Henry was crowned as King Henry VI of England in Westminster Abbey. That was a glorious occasion. Crowds came out to welcome their young king as he processed through London, hoping that this would herald a glorious reign.

Two years later, Henry was crowned king at Notre Dame in Paris. Although Reims Cathedral was the traditional site for the coronation of French kings, this wasn't possible for Henry as Reims lay in part of France which was controlled by Charles VII. At that time however, the English controlled Paris.

Henry was disappointed at the poor turnout in Paris to greet him on his coronation and the muted reaction of the sparse crowd. His uncle, Humphrey, explained that the French had mixed allegiance. In spite of the provision of the Treaty of Troyes, many regarded Charles VII as their rightful king and resented being ruled from

England by a king who couldn't speak their language.

"Well then, I must see to it that I learn to speak French," responded Henry.

French lessons were arranged and it wasn't long before Henry was fluent in the language of his other kingdom.

Chapter 3

The Queen

On his visits to Winchester with his uncle, Cardinal Beaufort, Henry had been impressed with the school which William of Wykeham had founded nearly a century earlier and he endorsed William's concept of providing education for the poor. Each year, seventy poor boys were admitted to the school. William of Wykeham had also founded New College at Oxford University, where successful pupils were expected to complete their education. So impressed was Henry with this school that one of Henry's first acts on reaching his majority was to found Eton College, on the other side of the River Thames to his home at Windsor Castle and he also founded King's College at Cambridge University. He invited a senior teacher from Winchester College, William Westbury, to be the first headmaster of his new school. William had greatly impressed Henry with his vision for the boys' education and the roles they could fulfil in society on completing their education. Like Winchester, Eton had provision for the admission of seventy boys from low income families. A similar number of students were admitted to King's College. Henry was particularly concerned that these institutes of learning should have lovely chapels and engaged the best architects he could find to design them. The chapel of King's College was not completed until well after Henry's death but he would have greatly appreciated this chapel as one of England's most beautiful churches.

Meanwhile, his uncles turned their attention to arranging a suitable marriage for Henry. As always, royal marriages had a political dimension and the current situation made the establishment of peace between England and France a prime objective in arranging such a match. England was faring badly in the ongoing hostilities. The French had learnt lessons from their reverses earlier in the war. No longer must English archers be allowed to control the outcome of battles as they had at Crecy and Agincourt. The archers had to be dealt with before they could wreak havoc with the French cavalry. Thus, at Patay, the English rear guard of archers was destroyed before the French resumed their pursuit of the retreating English army under Lod Talbot. The French were now acquiring artillery and the English had no match for this weapon. Establishing a lasting peace was deemed essential.

William de la Pole, the Earl of Suffolk, was identified as an ambassador who had the charm and personality necessary to negotiate a successful royal match but the task did not prove easy. Accompanied by Cardinal Beaufort, the Earl's first attempt to arrange a marriage with the daughter of Albert II, the king of a minor German state, failed. Albert probably feared entering an alliance which might take him into conflict with France, a more militarily powerful neighbour. Peace was made with Scotland which was allied to the French and the hand of the daughter of James I was sought but this was refused. An approach made to Charles VII in an attempt to marry Henry to one of his daughters failed because the English negotiators were not prepared to renounce Henry's claim to the French throne. They were nearly successful in arranging a match between Henry and one of the Count of Armagnac's daughter. However, this failed because the Count of Armagnac, who was at odds with the French royal house of Valois, became frightened when Charles VII mounted a massive attack against Gascony.

The ambassadors next approached Rene, the Duke of Anjou, with a view to arranging a marriage with his daughter, Margaret. The Duke had other impressive titles, notably those of King of Naples, King of Sicily and King of Jerusalem, but these titles were really meaningless. He has been described as a man with any crowns but no kingdoms. When they first met Margaret, who was then a girl in her late teens, the Earl of Suffolk and Cardinal Beaufort were awestruck at her breath-taking beauty. They discussed the marriage in early May and Margaret and her father were in favour of the match. However, knowing that an important part of the arrangement was the establishment of peace with France, permission was sought from Charles VII who was Margaret's uncle.

Margaret was furious that King Charles had to be involved.

"What right does this bastard son of Charles VI have to approve or disapprove my marriage arrangements," she stormed. "He calls himself king and has got himself crowned but as an illegitimate child, he has no right to the throne.

Henry is King of France. If my father is happy with the match, that should be sufficient."

The Earl of Suffolk and Cardinal Beaufort were secretly pleased to see such spirit in the girl. A wife like this was much needed by Henry to compensate for his diffident nature. Hard negotiations were carried out with King Charles and a fairly high price had to be paid to secure the match. It was finally agreed that the English would allow the French to take control of Maine, a province which had been in English possession. A two year truce between the English and French was agreed. The envoys knew that the concession of Maine would be unpopular in England but it was a price worth paying to enable Henry to marry this particular girl. By the end of May, the negotiations were complete and Margaret was formally betrothed to Henry by proxy. On their return to England, the negotiators initially kept secret the part of the deal which involved ceding Maine to the French.

Margaret arrived in England the following year and was enthusiastically greeted by the crowds in London as she made her ceremonial progress through the city. The following April, she married

King Henry at Titchfield Abbey in Hampshire and was crowned Queen of England by John Stafford, Archbishop of Canterbury, in Westminster Abbey at the end of May.

In spite of their very different temperaments, Henry and Margaret hit it off well. She was very much the dominant partner in the marriage. Using the way modern personality types are depicted, this was the successful marriage of an alpha woman with a gamma man, a combination which often proves surprisingly successful. Henry was enthralled with Margaret's beauty and Margaret really appreciated Henry's courteous and gentle nature, qualities sadly lacking in most men of the period. In the early years of their marriage, their common interest in education and culture helped cement their relationship. Margaret was impressed with the school and college that Henry had founded. Margaret's mother, the Countess Isabella of Lorraine, had ensured that her daughter received a good education. Having been well educated herself, Margaret was concerned that women didn't get the same opportunities for education as men. She would dearly have loved to establish a girls' equivalent of Eton but in the culture of the time, this wasn't possible.

However, she founded Queen's College, a sister college to Henry's King's College and, although originally restricted to male students, in the course of time and new enlightenment, there have been many notable female alumni of Queens' College. (Note the position of the apostrophe. Queen's College was re-founded by Margaret's rival Queen, Elizabeth Woodville, and thus became Queens' College!)

Eight years after their marriage, Henry and Elizabeth had a son, Edward of Westminster, Prince of Wales. Edward was his mother's pride and joy. He was spirited and showed every sign of becoming a great warrior as he entered his maturity.

Chapter 4

The Maid

Meanwhile, the war in France was progressing badly for England. Hostilities had resumed after the two year truce which had been agreed by the Treaty of Tours. This treaty had emanated from the negotiations by which the marriage of Margaret and Henry was settled. French successes under the leadership of Joan of Arc, also known as the Maid of Orleans, had revitalised the French. However, Joan of Arc was captured by the Burgundians who were allied to the English at the siege of Compiegne. Being of peasant origin, Joan had no wealthy relatives who could afford to ransom her and Charles VII, now confident that he could succeed in the war without the help of Joan, made no attempt to ransom or rescue her.

The Burgundians therefore handed Joan over to the English and she was taken to Rouen. There, Pierre Cauchon, Bishop of Beauvais and member of the English Council at Rouen, put Joan on trial. What followed could be described as no more than a mock trial. Rules of testimony, procedure and ecclesiastical law were completely disregarded. Joan was denied the right to a legal adviser and the tribunal was stacked entirely with pro-English clergy. Joan complained that all those present were hostile to her. Her request for ecclesiastics with French sympathies to be included to ensure impartiality was denied. The Vice Inquisitor of Northern France, Jean Lemaitre, was threatened with his life when he objected to the trial at the outset.

In spite of being an illiterate peasant, Joan amazed the court at her ability to evade the theological pitfalls in the loaded questions which her inquisitors had set to entrap her.

One interrogator asked her, "Do you know you're in God's grace?"

Joan replied, "If I am not, may God put me there; and if I am, may God so keep me. I should be the saddest creature in the world if I knew I were not in God's grace."

Her interrogators were stupefied by the cleverness of this answer, so neatly evading the pitfall they had set. Had Joan asserted that she was in God's grace, she would have been charged with heresy because the church doctrine of the day held that no one could be certain of being in God's grace. On the other hand, an answer that she wasn't in God's grace would have been taken as a confession of her own guilt.

Several members of the tribunal later testified that important portions of the court transcript were falsified, alterations being made in Joan's disfavour. She was confined in a secular prison guarded by English soldiers, contrary to inquisitional guidelines which required her to be confined in an ecclesiastical prison under the supervision of female guards. These would have been nuns. Bishop Cauchon denied Joan's right to appeal to the Council of Basel and to the Pope which would have certainly stopped the proceeding.

Cardinal Beaufort had asked Bishop Cauchon if he could be involved in the trial. The Bishop of Beauvais refused on the grounds that although part of England's ruling council, he was not part of the ruling council in France. Henry Beaufort was able to be present at the trial in Rouen and was allowed to visit Joan in prison He formed the impression that she was totally innocent of the charges levelled against her. Indeed, the only charge made which didn't seem to be in question was that Joan had been involved in cross dressing. This may seem a very trivial offence but was taken seriously in mediaeval times. In Joan's case, there were valid legal reasons why cross dressing should not be regarded as improper. If involved in a battle situation, it was permissible to wear armour which might well be regarded as unisex rather than male clothing. While in prison, male clothing provided some protection against rape which she was able to demonstrate was necessary in a prison staffed purely by ill-disciplined soldiers.

The odds were stacked against Joan. The outcome was predetermined. Joan was found guilty and sentenced to death. The sentence was carried out by burning her to death in the centre of Rouen.

When Cardinal Beaufort returned to England, Henry and Margaret were appalled by what had taken place in the name of English justice. Cardinal Beaufort said that he was so impressed by the saintliness of Joan that he would have a statue of Joan erected near the plot reserved for his tomb in Winchester Cathedral. That statue can be seen there to this day.

In spite of the loss of Joan's leadership as a result of her judicial murder, the war had turned its course in favour of the French. Apart from a minor victory of the English against a combined French and Scottish army at the battle of Herrings, the French inflicted a series of defeats on the English. The battles of Jargeau, Meung-sur-Loire, Beaugency, Patay and Gerbercy were all crushing French victories. In 1449, they took Rouen, the site of Joan's execution. This was followed by the Battle of Formigny during which there were over 4,000 English casualties and the capture of the English general, Thomas Kyriel. The final battle took place at Castillon where 4,000 English soldiers including John Talbot, Earl of Shrewsbury, the seasoned commander of the English army, and his son were killed.

This was effectively the end of the Hundred Years War. The only town in France remaining in English possession was Calais. On receiving this devastating news, King Henry suffered a severe nervous breakdown. Henry had previously shown signs of mental instability and this was attributed to a genetic trait inherited from his maternal grandfather, Charles VI, who had also been known as 'Charles, the Mad'.

Cardinal Beaufort commented, "Sadly, it would appear that the title, 'King of France' which Henry inherited from his grandfather, Charles VI, is now as meaningless as the royal titles held by Margaret's father, the Duke of Anjou, and the other thing that Henry has inherited from that grandfather is a mental health problem which is a far more serious affliction.

Great as was the victory at Agincourt which the English won against all odds, in the end, it has proved no more than a Pyrrhic victory!"

Chapter 5

<u>The Duke</u>

During and after the failure of a military campaign, recriminations are rife. Scapegoats are sought. Even before the final series of defeats when the provinces, previously won by Henry V, were lost as the English were pushed back to Caen, the Dukes of Gloucester and York were furious at the conduct of the war. In particular, they were angry that Maine had been ceded to the French. Possession of Maine was essential for the defence of Normandy. Their fury was chiefly directed against William de la Pole, Earl of Suffolk, who had made this concession by the Treaty of Tours. William, who had been largely responsible for arranging the marriage of Henry and Margaret was a great favourite with the Queen and she vigorously defended him. There was a really serious falling out between Queen Margaret and Richard, Duke of York.

"The country made a very poor bargain when they traded the kingdom of France for you," Richard sourly commented to Margaret. "The lords are appalled by the loss of their lands and the associated incomes for such a meagre recompense."

Margaret bristled at this comment and was understandably roused to anger.

"I was certainly not traded for the kingdom of France. France was lost because of the inept military performance of the troops under the command of people like yourself. It's not just your incompetent military leadership which is at fault. You're failing to read the signs of the times. The feudal system has run its course. In this country, the enlightened landowners are transforming the way their property is owned so that those you regard as no more than serfs become tenant farmers with a real incentive for making the best of their land. They're not a private army waiting to be mobilised every time a lord wants to steal his neighbour's property. In France, the peasants are still treated as serfs. Had they been treated better by you English landlords, they'd have fought far more effectively and seen off Charles' challenge. The greed of the English lords contributed to the loss of France in no small way. Mark my words, if the aristocracy in France continue to treat the peasants living on their estates the way they do, one day there will be such an uprising in France that the lords will rue the fact that they treated the peasants so badly!"

The Duke of York had been in command in France but he was sent to govern Ireland instead and the Duke of Somerset, who had been recently promoted from being just an earl, was sent to command affairs in France where the situation was getting steadily worse for the English. Somerset had clashed with Gloucester over the conduct of the war and the now elderly Duke of Gloucester was imprisoned at Bury St. Edmunds where he died soon after his imprisonment.

The defeat in France was exacerbating a problem which already existed in parts of England where laws were being disregarded. Large numbers of soldiers returning from France were seeking employment. These were recruited by some of the less scrupulous English aristocracy to augment their existing private armies which they were using to take over their neighbours' property.

The Duke of York was not the only one who identified the Duke of Suffolk as the source of England's woes. Suffolk who became referred to by the derisive nickname, Jackanapes, was impeached by Parliament. This time, Queen Margaret could not protect her favourite and he was sent into exile. However, he was murdered on the ship conducting him abroad and his body was found on the beach near Dover.

Meanwhile, the Duke of York was persuaded by lords in the north to return from Ireland to put an end to the bad government. He raised an army at Shrewsbury and made an alliance with the Earl of Warwick, the most powerful lord in England. He confronted and defeated the army loyal to King Henry at St. Albans and took his place on the governing council of England where he was appointed 'Protector of England'. Queen Margaret was excluded from the Council and Cardinal Beaufort was imprisoned in the Tower of London.

This was the state of England encountered at the beginning of this book where Baron Howard was able to steal Baron de Ros's cattle with impunity. Hr knew that as he had supported Richard, Duke of York, at St. Albans, he would be favoured by Richard of York who now held the real power in the land, over one who had supported Henry.

The King had been slightly wounded in the battle of St. Alban's but it hadn't really been a big affair. However, there was a grave danger of the country relapsing into civil was which no-one really wanted. The Archbishop of Canterbury, Thomas Bouchier, realised that a serious attempt at reconciliation was needed and he persuaded the King to arrange a 'love day'. The two opposing factions were identified as Lancaster and York. This was in view of Henry's direct descent from John of Gaunt, Duke of Lancaster, and York was the title of Richard's duchy. The two sides had adopted roses as their emblem, red for Lancaster and white for York. Principal members of both factions walked hand in hand in pairs to St. Paul's Cathedral where a service of reconciliation was held. Recognising his unpopularity in London, Henry set up his court in Coventry.

The truce may have lasted had nothing happened to precipitate further conflict. However, the Duke of York's ally, the Earl of Warwick who held the title, Captain of Calais, the last English possession in France, started to harass neutral ships, both from the Hanseatic League and Spain. These diplomatic incidents resulted in Warwick being recalled to Coventry to explain himself to the King. Warwick could have no justifiable explanation for his action. Fearing the outcome of an appearance before the king in the absence of his supporters when he could well have been arrested and attainted, Warwick arranged with York's other main supporter, the Earl of Salisbury, to join the Duke of York at Ludlow. The Lancastrians, seeing the danger of this coalition, attempted to prevent Salisbury from reaching Ludlow in a battle fought at Blore Heath but the Lancastrians lost this battle.

Recognising the danger of this concentration of Yorkist forces, the Lancastrians assembled a large army and defeated the smaller combined armies of York, Warwick and Salisbury at Ludford Bridge. The defeated Duke of York fled to Ireland which had been under his control in the past. York, Warwick and Salisbury raised another army which they landed in Kent knowing that the Duke of York was widely supported in the south and specially in London. They gained further support as they marched on Northampton where they defeated the Lancastrians. King Henry was captured but Queen Margaret escaped and fled to

Wales where she knew she could count on Lancastrian support.

By now, the stakes had been raised. York wanted more than the title of Protector of England. As he was the direct descendent of Edward III's second son, the Duke of Clarence, and Henry was directly descended from Edward III's third son, John of Gaunt, Duke of Lancaster, he considered that his claim to the throne was better than Henry's. Richard's descent had come through a female line, Clarence's daughter, Philippa, Countess of Ulster, but this shouldn't have been an obstacle to his claim. The Law of Primogeniture worked differently in England than in France. Precedent for inheriting the crown through a female line had already been set by Henry II whose mother, Matilda, was the only daughter of Henry I. The country was not prepared to depose Henry at that stage but Parliament accepted the claim represented by the Duke of York's royal lineage. Parliament therefore decided that the Duke of York should be recognised as Henry's successor, thereby disinheriting Henry's son, Edward, Prince of Wales.

This is something that Queen Margaret would definitely not have accepted but she was away, first in Wales and then in Scotland, raising armies to regain control of England. In Scotland, she struck up a friendship with the Queen of Scotland, Mary of Guelders, consort to James II. Mary consented to give Margaret the troops she needed in return for ceding Berwick on Tweed to Scotland and arranging for the betrothal of her daughter, Margaret, to Edward, Prince of Wales. Queen Margaret agreed to these terms and returned to England with an army where she encountered York's army at Wakefield.

Queen Margaret, resplendent in shiny army, paraded herself before her army outside Wakefield.

"Loyal subjects," she started, her voice ringing out clearly over her assembled troops, "our country is being taken over by an upstart rebel who is holding your king in captivity and lording himself as Protector of England. This popinjay is no such thing. He's a carpet knight, just a jumped-up opportunist who is prepared to shed English blood in pursuit of his ambition."

Margaret spat out her bitter rhetoric.

"The Duke of York was released from imprisonment on his undertaking that he wouldn't take up arms against his lawful king and look at what he's done. I call upon you, valiant soldiers, to fight bravely today and rid this realm of the canker which is destroying the peace and prosperity which this nation deserves after the traumas it has experienced in recent years. Fight bravely then for your King, for your Queen and for England!" she concluded as she brandished her sword.

Margaret's rousing speech with which she rallied her army was greeted with enthusiastic cheers from the assembled troops. Her army went on to win the battle of Wakefield. News came to Margaret at the end of the battle that the Duke of York had been killed.

"Hopefully, this marks the beginning of the end of our problems," thought Margaret but her optimism was misplaced. A greater threat was looming in the form of York's son, Edward, whose ambition was to claim the crown for himself.

Further battles were to ensue. The Yorkists defeated the army of Jasper Tudor, a Lancastrian sympathiser, at Mortimer's Cross. However, the Lancastrians reversed this defeat at the second battle fought at St. Alban's when they were able to release King Henry. A month later, the Yorkists regained supremacy by defeating the Lancastrians at Ferrybridge. After this battle, York's son, Edward, had himself proclaimed King Edward IV. Things then started to move quickly. Both sides assembled large armies and they met a month later at Towton in Yorkshire for a great showdown.

Chapter 6

The Battle of Towton

News came to Baron de Ros that the Queen had raised her standard at Tadcaster in preparation for meeting a Yorkist army which was heading up from the south. De Ros, with the few men he could muster, travelled south from Helmsley to join the Queen's forces. Lady Philippa insisted on travelling with her husband on this mission. She was accompanied by her maid, Constance. When they neared Tadcaster, Lady Philippa and Constance put up at the Swan, an inn in Bramham, just west of Tadcaster while the Baron went on to join the Queen. Meanwhile, Edward's army set up their camp at Sherburn-in-Elmet. At break of day, the two huge armies struck camp and moved towards each other. The sky was dark, presaging the bad weather which was about to break.

Approximately three quarters of English peers were included among the two armies, eight with the Yorkist army and at least nineteen with the Lancastrians. Of the Yorkist faction, the Duke of Norfolk was deemed too old to participate in the battle, and the Earl of Warwick was absent, having suffered a leg wound in the recent battle at Ferrybridge. However, Norfolk's contingent, commanded by Walter Blount, and Warwick's, commanded by his uncle, Lord Fauconberg, were available to fight in the battle about to ensue. Fauconberg was a highly regarded and experienced veteran who had commanded the Yorkist vanguard at the Battle of Northampton. The Lancastrian army was commanded by Henry Beaufort, Duke of Somerset, an experienced leader who had won victories at Wakefield and St. Alban's. Other Lancastrian leaders included the Duke of Exeter, the Earl of Northumberland, Lord Ralph Dacre and of course, Baron de Ros.

The two armies met on a plateau between the villages of Saxton and Towton. The steeply banked Cock Beck flowed in an S-shaped course around the plateau. The Lancastrians arrived at the site first and the Duke of Somerset made the seemingly sound decision to deploy his troops on the plateau which would block any enemy advance towards the city of York. They were protected from flanking attacks by a deep valley to the south and marshes around the Cock Beck to the right. No sooner had Somerset deployed his troops than the Yorkist army arrived, huge lines of troops lining up on the crest of the ridge opposite the Lancastrians. The Yorkists were outnumbered as Norfolk's troops had yet to arrive to join the force.

Although the battle took place in the early days of Spring on 29th March which was Palm Sunday, the weather was far from good for the time of the year as the Lancastrian and Yorkist armies confronted each other. This proved a decisive factor in the battle as a strong wind got up from behind the Yorkist army and it began to snow. Somerset's plan had been to stand his ground and wait for the smaller Yorkist army come to him. However, realising the advantage to be derived from a strong tail wind, Fauconberg ordered his archers to come forward and unleash a volley of arrows towards the Lancastrians located at just about at the maximum range of a longbow. The wind allowed the arrows to travel further than usual and caused heavy casualties among the Lancastrian ranks. The answering volley from the Lancastrians fired against the wind proved ineffective, falling short of their target and leaving a carpet of arrows in front of the Yorkists whose archers had been ordered to step back, having fired their murderous opening volley. The Yorkist archers were able to rearm themselves with the Lancastrian arrows as they advanced later in the battle. Blinded by the blizzard blowing against them, the Lancastrians were unaware that their salvo had fallen short. They continued firing until they ran out of ammunition. Fauconberg then ordered his archers forward and they fired into the Lancastrians with the arrows they picked up from the ground as they advanced. The Lancastrian archers now had no effective response. The Lancastrian army then moved forward to engage the Yorkists in close combat. The archers moved behind the protective rank of armoured men leading the advance. Somerset ordered his cavalry to attack the left wing of the Yorkist army which began to fall into disarray until Edward took charge and rallied the troops. As they met, the Yorkist archers fired into the Lancastrians at short range but the numerical superiority of the Lancastrians caused the Yorkists to give ground.

The fighting continued for three hours, the Lancastrians gradually gaining the advantage until Norfolk's army at last arrived on the scene, decisively shifting the balance of power. The

Lancastrians continued to fight but by the end of the day, their line had broken into small groups. Seeing the hopelessness of their situation, they began to flee for their lives. The combat had lasted for ten hours. The fleeing Lancastrians threw off their armour to enable them to run faster but were vulnerable to the fresher troops from Norfolk's forces who had arrived later in the battle and could outrun them. Edward had ordered his pursuing troops to spare the soldiers but kill the nobles. He was aware that the soldiers were not political opponents but merely serfs obeying their feudal overlords. However, having lost so many of their colleagues in the battle, the Yorkists were in no mood to spare anyone and the Lancastrians were cut down from behind and even killed after they had surrendered. Forty-two knights were executed after they had been taken prisoner.

The Lancastrians suffered more casualties in their rout than they had done on the actual battlefield. Not all were killed by the pursuing Yorkists but had drowned as they tried to cross the Cock Beck and the much wider River Wharfe. The few bridges over these rivers had collapsed under the weight of men trying to cross them and the

Lancastrians eventually found themselves crossing the rivers over the 'dams' of dead bodies of their colleagues clogging the streams. Some actually reached Tadcaster and York but were hunted down and killed.

Good contemporary records of the battle are not available so an accurate figure of the casualties cannot be given. A news brief, widely circulated a few days after the battle, reported a figure of 28,000 dead, 20,000 Lancastrians and 8,000 Yorkists. These figures, which are commensurate with the casualties suffered on First World War battlefields, make Towton by far the bloodiest battle fought on English soil. The Earl of Northumberland and Lord Dacre had been killed in the battle. The Earls of Devon and Wiltshire were captured and executed. The only notable aristocrat on the Yorkist side to be killed in the battle was Lord Horne.

On hearing news of the defeat of the Lancastrian army, King Henry, Queen Margaret and Prince Edward fled into exile in Scotland. They were later joined by the Dukes of Somerset and Exeter and a few other lords who had escaped the battle.

Several of the gentry who had supported Edward were elevated to the peerage and Lord Fauconberg was created Earl of Kent. The Earl of Warwick received parts of Northumberland to add to the extensive estates he already held and was made King's Lieutenant in the North and Admiral of the English fleet. Thus, Warwick's considerable influence and power was further increased.

Meanwhile, on hearing the result of the battle, Philippa de Ros sent Lady Constance to find out what had happened to her husband.

Chapter 7

The Lollards

Nearly a century before the events related in this story, John Wycliffe, a learned theologian from Oxford University, had seriously challenged the way the church was being run and the teaching it was giving.

Wycliffe did not accept the Catholic Church's view of ***transubstantiation***, that is that on its consecration, the elements used in communion change from being bread and wine into the actual body and blood of Christ. This doctrine was held to be so important by the Catholic Church that denial of this belief was regarded as extreme heresy. Wycliffe held the self-evident opinion that the bread and wine remained as such but embodied the real presence of Christ insofar as they enriched the recipient who received them in good faith with the full benefits of Christ's redeeming sacrifice. This doctrine was known as ***consubstantiation***.

Wycliffe maintained that the only basis for Christian doctrine should be Holy Scripture and not church tradition. He was not satisfied that either the doctrines of the church or the preaching of the clergy of his day were true to scripture. This being the case, Wycliffe saw the need to produce a translation of the Bible into English as spoken at the time. He therefore translated the Bible from the version in Latin called the Vulgate, into an English language edition. This Bible would enable God's Word to be independently accessed by literate people without their need to know Latin or Greek.

Wycliffe didn't approve of the church practices of praying to the saints and honouring their images. This he regarded as idolatry. He considered the church's accumulation of wealth to be corrupt. Offering prayers for the dead and the setting up chantries by prominent churchmen where prayers could be said for their souls after their death, was further evidence of this corruption. He believed these practices had no scriptural basis and distracted priests from other more important work such as directing their prayers towards the living where there was a more immediate need for prayer. Many priests were in post as a result of their relationship with the local lord rather than by virtue of their learning. They benefitted financially from the tithes and rents paid like taxes on land owned by the church. Wycliffe rejected the value of papal pardons and considered confession to a priest to be unnecessary as he didn't consider priests had the authority to forgive sins. Neither did he advocate the restrictions imposed by the Catholic Church for fasting and abstinence. Wycliffe challenged the practice of clerical celibacy and upheld the concept of the priesthood of all believers.

Had Caxton's press in England been as efficient as the Gutenberg press in Germany and Wycliffe's Bible been more widely circulated, Wycliffe rather than Luther might well have been credited as the one who launched the reformation. Wycliffe's teaching strongly influenced other later continental reformers like Jan Huss in Bohemia, Huldrych Zwingli in Switzerland and John Calvin in France, so that Wycliffe has rightly been referred to as 'the Morning Star of the Reformation'.

Wycliffe's teaching had a very mixed reception. It was fiercely opposed by many in the church who had a vested interest in the status quo and felt threatened by Wycliffe's teaching. It was tolerated at Oxford University on the basis that the University encouraged an atmosphere of academic freedom. It was supported by many men of influence, including John of Gaunt, Duke of Lancaster, which went some way to protecting adherents to Wycliffe's preaching from being persecuted by the church.

Wycliffe commissioned many so called ordinary men who didn't have the benefit of a university education but who, nonetheless, were inspired by the Holy Spirit, to travel round the country as itinerant preachers, chiefly expounding Holy Scripture but also drawing attention to Wycliffe's teaching on matters where the existing church was in need of reform. These 'ordinary men' were known as Lollards. They dressed in a distinctive habit so that they could be identified by the population at large as *religieux*. This was a term which included priests, friars, monks, nuns and others who wore clerical habit. As they travelled round the country, Lollards had a mixed reception. They were not welcome by most parish priests to preach in their churches but they gathered enthusiastic crowds at open air meetings who were greatly moved at their their inspired preaching. These congregations particularly enjoyed hearing readings from Wycliffe's Bible, rendered in their own language.

Two such Lollards were Matthew and Michael who had experienced the vocation to become itinerant preachers after hearing Lollards preach in the village where they were brought up. Both were good looking young men but of the two, Matthew was the more handsome while Michael was the more eloquent preacher. Like the missionary disciples in the gospels, they travelled the country as a pair. They first sought permission of the local priests to preach in their churches. This was often refused but some of the more enlightened clergy welcomed the refreshing message proclaimed with such eloquence by these Lollards. More often than not, they had to preach their message in the open air and they invariably attracted a sizeable crowd who listened enthusiastically to preaching which was usually more powerful than that delivered by their parish priest. They always received offerings of lodging for the night at a home in the village where they were conducting their ministry.

One Palm Sunday, they were in Ulleskelf in Yorkshire where the enlightened parish priest, the

Prebendary Richard Hayman, had welcomed them to preach at his church of St. Peter's. The conversation turned to a battle which was believed to be taking place that day. Indeed, many of the villagers claimed they had heard the shouting and the screams from the battlefield. By evening, two bedraggled Lancastrian soldiers who had evaded capture from pursuing Yorkists entered the village seeking help. Richard was not partisan to either of the Rose's factions but concerned mainly to be able to offer succour to the needy. He invited them into his vicarage where they met Matthew and Michael who had no great interest in the outcome of the civil war taking place but were interested to hear these men's story. They had minor wounds which Peter's wife dressed before providing them with much needed food. Soldiers involved in the thick of a battle are not often aware of the big picture of what is happening over the total battlefield but these Lancastrians gave a pretty good account of what had happened and the crucial way weather had affected the outcome.

The following day, Richard welcomed the soldiers to remain a little longer until they felt recovered. They declared themselves fit enough to travel to their homes where they knew their families would be anxiously waiting for news but they asked to stay another day at the vicarage by which time the Yorkists would have dispersed and it would be safer to travel. Matthew and Michael bade their farewell to Richard and his wife, wished the recovering Lancastrian soldiers well and made their way to the battlefield to ascertain what help if any they might be able to give to any wounded who remained on the battlefield..

They sky was still overcast as Matthew and Michael started their quest. They were hardly prepared for the horror they were about to encounter. Even before reaching the battlefield, they encountered the mutilated bodies of men who had been hacked to death by their pursuers as they fled the field. When they reached the site of the battle, they were appalled to see thousands of dead sprawled across the field, some with limbs hacked off, others with arrows still protruding from their body. Carrion birds were pecking at the corpses. Ghoulish crones were wondering about the field, seeking anything of value, if not actual money, which they could cannibalize, perhaps a knife or a leather belt.

They were even stripping anything which looked serviceable, even if blood-stained, like clothing from the bodies. Every body they encountered was dead and beyond any succour that Matthew or Michael could provide. Then they saw a younger woman who was obviously trying to help a wounded soldier and they made their way over to see if they could be of assistance. The woman was Lady Constance who was trying to bind the wounds of a barely conscious but living soldier. This was Lord Thomas de Ros. Matthew and Michael offered their help and Lady Constance asked if they could help her transport her Lord back to Bramham where her mistress was lodging at an inn. Constance completed dressing de Ros's wound while the Lollards set about constructing a makeshift stretcher. They found two lances abandoned on the field and using the spare clothing they always carried with them, constructed a serviceable stretcher. They then set off on the slow journey to Bramham, the task becoming a little easier once they had negotiated the dead bodies lying around them and made the road.

After several hours, they reached the Swan in Bramham. Lady Philippa was naturally concerned that her husband had been wounded but so relieved that he was alive. She was very grateful too, of course to Constance, but also to these Lollards without whom, Baron de Ros would never have made the journey to Bramham. The fact that the Baron had been wounded in the battle was a blessing in disguise. Had he fled from the scene, it was almost certain that he would have either been hacked down by the pursuing Yorkists or captured and executed which was the fate of other captured Lancastrian lords.

It was clear that the Baron would not be fit to travel back to Helmsley for a few days and would have to stay in the relative safety of the inn. Matthew and Michael were welcomed to stay with them. Lady Philippa realised that being accompanied by the two Lollards would make their return to Helmsley safer.

Chapter 8

Helmsley Castle

After a few days' rest, Thomas de Ros felt fit enough to make the journey home to Helmsley on horseback, a journey not without its dangers as groups of Yorkist soldiers might have identified the Baron as a fugitive from the battle. However, such fears were unfounded. Travelling slowly along the road, the Baron and ladies on horseback and the Lollards on foot, they made Helmsley after a few hours without experiencing any hostile encounters on the way. Matthew and Michael were told that they were welcome to make Helmsley Castle their home until they felt the need to move on. The two Lollards were glad to accept this invitation. The castle would make an excellent base from which to launch their missionary activity.

The establishment at Helmsley Castle were glad to see their chatelains safely home but naturally concerned that Baron Thomas was wounded. Only a few of the men who had left Helmsley for Tadcaster where the Queen had raised her standard had returned safely and there were several grieving widows on the castle estates. Who would care for their cattle or bring in the harvest later that year? Matthew and Michael soon became aware of the problem and discussed a possible solution with Constance. She warmly accepted their ideas and shared their suggestions with her mistress who in turn talked with the Baron.

The idea involved taking a census of the population of the local estates, numbers broken down by gender and age and the degree of fitness of both men and women to carry out farm labouring jobs. The result was as expected. A number of smallholdings were identified with no male leadership. From this data and a knowledge of the positions of the various small farms, it was possible to group the farms into contiguous larger holdings, each with at least three fit men to take charge of organising the manual work. The produce of these holdings was to be shared among the various homes within the new farmsteads created, on a pro-rata basis according to the numbers dwelling in each home. Thomas de Ros enthusiastically agreed to the plan and held a meeting of his tenants where the idea was explained. There were no dissenting voices. The small holders were glad of the leadership being shown at a time when the community was facing significant problems.

Meanwhile, the Lollards were able to resume their preaching ministry. They were favourably received by the Reverend Will Hakford, Vicar of All Saints, Helmsley parish church, who welcomed them to share his pulpit. The congregations greatly appreciated hearing the Bible read in their own language and hearing the Lollards' sermons.

Matthew and Michael noticed a candle surrounded by a red glass shade in the sanctuary of the church and saw how Philip bowed or genuflected every time he passed the light. Matthew and Michael had seen such lights many times before and were well aware of what they represented. After they had established a good relationship of trust with the Vicar and recognizing that unlike so many of the clergy they had encountered, he was an intelligent open minded man, they asked him about the significance of this light. They were told, as they had expected, that this light indicated that in the nearby aumbry were the body and blood of Jesus in the form of the elements which had been consecrated at a service of Holy Communion. In line with the teaching of the church, he accepted that these elements had been transformed into the actual shed blood and part of the body of Jesus, broken on the cross. He argued on the lines that according to scripture, at the Last Supper, Jesus had declared the bread and wine shared to be his broken body and shed blood. The Lollards pointed out that at the Last Supper, Jesus body was intact, nothing had been broken and no blood spilt. Will Hakford paused in thought and the Lollards allowed him time to think this through. They knew full well that he would be aware that in reality, the consecrated bread remained as bread and so with the wine. After leaving time for reflection, they explained Wycliffe's doctrine of consubstantiation. The Reverend Will Hakford asked for time to think this through overnight. The next day, the Lollards were somewhat satisfied to see that the presence light, for this is the name given to such lamps, had been removed. They were tactful enough not to mention the matter again.

Each day, Matthew and Michael made excursions from the castle into the local area, largely restricting their forays to remain within the estate centred on Helmsley Castle. Some of the local vicars welcomed them into their churches but few were as accommodating as the Reverend Will Hakford had been. However, open air preaching and worship was their normal modus operandi and they invariably gathered intensely sincere and interested groups of worshippers joining them on the pitches where they set up. These services were invariably followed with one-to-one counselling where the Lollards could explain points of interest or challenge which had come up during their sermons in simple language and in greater depth.

In the evenings when they returned to the castle, Lord and Lady de Ros, Constance and other senior members of the castle establishment would delight in hearing passages from Wycliffe's Bible read by candle-light and Wycliffe's Christian doctrine, so firmly based in scripture, explained. Matthew and Michael discovered that while Constance and the de Ros's acknowledged Jesus as Saviour, they believed that final judgement would hinge on whether the good they had done in their lives outweighed the bad. They had not grasped the concept of salvation through the freely available grace. The Lollards had frequently encountered this misconception among those to whom they ministered. They explained that salvation could not be earned by good works as these would be more than counterbalanced by the sin which clings to all of us. They cited the example in the Bible where Jesus had told the rich young ruler that he needed to sell all his possessions, give them to the poor and follow him if he desired salvation. This was something the young man felt unable to do. Jesus then explained to his disciples that it was easier for a camel to pass through the eye of a needle than for a rich man to enter the kingdom of heaven! The disciples were surprised for, in their culture, it was believed that riches were a divinely bestowed gift on those whom God favoured and were therefore an indication that the salvation of a rich person was assured. They asked Jesus about their own destiny since they had given up all to follow him. They did not receive the answer they expected, that they had earned their salvation in doing this but Jesus told them that for man salvation was impossible, but everything was possible to God. It was not appropriate for Jesus to explain at that point how that salvation would come through, and only through, his sacrificial death.

Matthew and Michael continued by explaining that salvation was a free gift for those who recognised that Christ had taken the sin which clings to us all upon himself when he died upon the cross. It was available to all who were prepared to acknowledge what Christ had done in dying for them and who were prepared to commit their lives to him. In simple terms, this didn't mean struggling to obey laws of goodness and trying to accumulate a record of as many good works as possible. It meant recognising throughout their lives that henceforth they belonged to Christ and every thought or action, every decision made, should be what they thought Jesus would do in any situation in which they found themselves Hence, the need to study scripture to get to really know Jesus and what he stood for.

During the day, when her services were not required by Lady Philippa, Constance was busy providing help and support where she could to the needy on the Helmsley estate. For reasons of personal safety which were necessary in those times, she seldom rode alone and was usually accompanied by a soldier from the castle garrison. As his strength returned, Lord Thomas de Ros occasionally accompanied Constance himself on her sorties. Then, on one occasion, they had a serious misadventure. Constance and Thomas de Ros were making their way to the western part of the Helmsley estate to help a woman who was experiencing greater problems than usual after childbirth when they were suddenly surrounded by a group of soldiers who accused them of trespassing on the land belonging to Baron John Howard. Thomas de Ros protested vigorously that they were well within his own estate boundary but to no avail, the soldiers insisted on conducting them to John Howard's castle at Pickering. Thomas felt quite sure that John Howard had sent spies to observe his movements from Helmsley Castle and was awaiting an opportunity when he was close enough to Pickering Castle to have him captured.

Chapter 9

<u>Pickering Castle</u>

After a journey taking a few hours during which they forded the rivers Dove and Seven, they arrived at Pickering Castle, one of the strongholds held by Baron John Howard. A message had evidently been relayed to Baron Howard by his lookouts on the castle ramparts for when Thomas de Ros and Constance were ushered into the great hall, Baron John Howard was already seated on a throne like chair set on an elevated dais. He was richly dressed but his face which was framed by a black beard and raven hair, looked distinctly sinister. It wore a permanent scowl and he peered through ominously penetrating eyes.

"So what have we here, a fugitive from the battle of Towton and his slut of a mistress," he snarled, addressing them in a purposely insulting manner with his unfounded description of Constance. Baron Howard had proud memories of the battle of Towton as the new King Edward had knighted him after the victory had been won. "I should hand you over to King Edward so that he can arrange for you to experience the execution that you escaped at Towton. However, I am a merciful man and may be able to think of something better. You, Thomas de Ros, can spend a few days in a cell while you, young wench, can go and work in my kitchen. Take them away," the Baron commanded.

He immediately looked away and after a pause, left the dais to indicate that Thomas and Constance were now of no more immediate interest to him. Thomas de Ros was thus denied the right of reply or protest.

Baron Howard knew full well that the current preoccupation of the King was to reunite the country after the divisive civil war that had taken place. Now the heat of battle was well past, he would have no interest in executing a minor lord whose offence was no more than to serve the one he believed to be his rightful king and whose execution would revive antagonism towards himself. However, Baron de Ros and Constance would be unaware of the King's thinking.

Two soldiers led de Ros off in one direction and two more conducted Constance to the kitchen where it was clear her arrival was not unexpected.

She was met by a cheerful man whose smiling face was a complete contrast to that of Baron Howard. This was Robin Standing, the chief cook.

"Welcome to my kitchen," he beamed. "I was told that a young lady would be joining my staff. I hope that you'll enjoy working for me. I think you'll find I run a well-ordered kitchen. What's your name?"

On being told that she was called Constance, he called over a sweet looking serving maid.

"Alice, this is Constance. Can you show her around the kitchens, store houses and pantries."

Alice smiled warmly and the next hour was spent in exploring the kitchen and its associated storerooms and in being introduced to the other kitchen staff.

For the next couple of days, Constance was set to work in the kitchen. The tasks she was given weren't onerous or unpleasant. Constance was not a high-born lady but came from peasant stock and had no problem in coping with the tasks that came her way. Indeed, working there was quite a pleasant experience as her fellow workers were a jolly cooperative bunch who quickly enabled Constance to feel at home. They were sympathetic about the way she'd been brought to the castle. However, although he was clearly disliked, no-one dared say openly anything disrespectful about Baron John Howard.

Lord de Ros was taken out, through the castle courtyard to the base of one of the towers which punctuated the outer wall. There he was met by the one who was to become his jailer, Giles Noirmont. The etymology of his name meant that when out of earshot, he was always referred to as Black Giles, a name which matched his nature and his clothing rather than his hair and beard which were fair. If anything, he was almost more sinister than Baron Howard in appearance. One sensed that he had a very cruel streak in his nature.

"So you're the Lancastrian rebel who needs to be taught a lesson," he sneered. "Follow me and I'll show you to your lodging for the foreseeable future, that is, unless the king wants to make a quick end to the likes of people like you."

Black Giles was not the sort of person you argue with. Baron de Ros followed Giles up a narrow spiral stairway which issued on to a small landing. Giles ushered de Ros into a small room with not much more than a bed for furniture and slammed the door. There was no keyhole but de Ros heard bolts being operated from the outside. Thomas de Ros could survey the world outside the castle from a small, barred, unglazed window.

Constance would have enjoyed working in the kitchen and getting to know her fellow workers were it not for the involuntary nature of her confinement. She tried to find out as much as she could regarding Thomas de Ros's situation from her fellow workers who had quickly grown to like Constance. Her new friends were quite upset about the situation in which she and Thomas de Ros now found themselves. They were able to let her know that Thomas was confined in a room in one of the towers. When she enquired if they thought she would be able to see the Thomas, they told her that her master's jailer, Black Giles, occupied a room at the base of the tower where he stood guard and would never let her pass.

"However", they said, "the room can be approached from above by walking along the outer wall of the castle, easily accessible from any of the other towers in the wall, and entering the imprisonment tower through a door at the top of the tower. They were sure that this door was never kept locked. Thomas would be imprisoned in a room below this. Thus, his cell could be accessed by the spiral staircase which was the way up and down every tower in the castle."

Guided by one of the kitchen maids, Constance was able to reach the door of the room where the Baron was imprisoned. She noticed that the door was only bolted but there was no point in opening the door then as she had no plan of what next step might be taken to get him safely out of the castle. For fear of being heard by Black Giles on the floor below, she could only speak softly through the door but the short conversation was sufficient for each of them to be aware that for the time being they were both all right. Constance knew she had to return quickly to the kitchen to avoid her absence being noticed by someone who might report this to John Howard.

After a couple of days, Constance was summoned to appear before Baron John Howard.

"As I declared when we first met," started Baron John, "I'm a merciful man and don't want to send your master to the King to face certain execution. I'm prepared to release your master but require a ransom of £ 10,000 to be paid."

Quoting an actual figure in terms of the value of modern currency is meaningless in view of the vast inflation which has taken place over the centuries. Needless to say, the sum demanded was vast in terms of the coinage of the day and would be very difficult to raise.

"Besides being a man of mercy, I'm also patient. The money can be paid in instalments but mark my words, de Ros won't be released until every last penny has been paid. You're to be my messenger to convey this demand to Lady de Ros. I expect you back by this time tomorrow or I'll assume my request has been denied and I'll dispatch Thomas de Ros to the King."

Constance was set off on her messenger journey on the horse she had been riding when she arrived at Pickering Castle but no escort was provided. Some hours later, she arrived back at Helmsley where Philippa de Ros had been beside herself with anxiety. She was relieved to see Constance and to learn that Thomas was still alive but dismayed by his circumstances and the ransom demand.

"We can never raise that sort of money," she wailed.

Constance had been impressed at the resourcefulness of the Lollards and she felt sure that they might have some idea of how to deal with the situation. When they returned to the castle from their day's missionary activities, Constance told them about the situation in which the de Ros's now found themselves. Matthew and Michael's immediate response was to get Philippa to join the three of them for a time of prayer. After about half or maybe three quarters of an hour, Matthew asked them if God had spoken to them during that period.

Michael said that an idea had come to him as he pondered on the fact that Thomas's cell was accessible without passing Black Giles and that the door was not locked but only bolted on the outside. He asked Constance how easy it would be for Matthew and himself to enter Pickering Castle.

"That shouldn't be a problem," Constance told them. "Although there are two guards on the door, the main purpose is to stop any who might be seen as an armed insurgent. Traders are coming in and out all the time with provisions for the castle. I have seen monks and nuns, presumably on holy business, enter and leave the castle without being challenged so a pair of religieux like yourself should be able to get in easily."

"Well then," said Michael, "I suggest that Matthew and myself come to the castle for a few days to look round and get to know the lie of the land, in particular, the tower in which the Baron is being confined and the way to access the Baron's cell from the outer wall. We can centre our missionary activity for the time being in Pickering. There'll be someone there who'll grant us free lodging. As we become fully acquainted with the situation in the castle, we'll be able to identify a day when we can put into operation a rescue plan which came to me as we prayed."

He elaborated his plan.

"On the day of the rescue, Matthew and I would enter the castle separately at a well-spaced interval. One of us will go to the Baron's cell, approaching it from the curtain wall and following the route you used, Constance. We'll carry a spare Lollard habit and a razor in my travel bag. After shaving, Thomas should change into the habit and put his own clothes into the bag. We'll then make our way back to the courtyard and thence leave the castle. I'll leave first, the Baron following after a well-spaced interval, and lastly, Matthew after a further interval. It's unlikely that the guards will have counted the number of Lollards coming in and out of the castle but if they have and challenge a third Lollard leaving the castle, having noticed that only two entered, they'll find that the third Lollard, Matthew, is entirely genuine."

They applauded this idea. It was simple and that made it all the more likely to work.

"When should this plan be put into effect?" asked Lady Philippa.

Matthew suggested that once all the reconnaissance had been carried out, they should look for a day when something was taking place in the castle which would create a diversion. This would increase the chance of their being able to leave the main courtyard and move around undetected into parts of the castle where they wouldn't normally be expected to be. Constance suggested an easily identifiable place by a thicket out of sight of the castle where she could rendezvous with the Lollards the following Tuesday afternoon. There she could update them on anything happening in the castle which would create such a diversion. She knew that she couldn't be precise in stating a time for this meeting as this would depend on the duties imposed on her in the kitchen, but she seemed to be no more restricted in her movements around and in and out of the castle than other workers. This was because Baron John Howard knew that Constance would be jeopardising her master's life if she tried to escape.

The following morning, Constance returned to the castle, this time escorted by a soldier from the Helmsley garrison, up to the thicket from which

Pickering Castle was just in view. The soldier then kept watch from this site which couldn't be easily observed from the Castle until he could see through the trees that Constance was safely in the Castle. He then returned to Helmsley. Constance reported to John Howard that Lady Philippa was prepared to pay the ransom by instalments but would need a little time even to raise an acceptable first instalment. She then returned to her work in the kitchen.

Chapter 10

The Escape

An unwelcome situation soon arose but one which would create the required diversion. Baron John Howard was extremely ill with dysentery. It was no secret that many in the castle establishment hoped that this would prove fatal but that was not to be. John Howard made a fairly rapid recovery. The fact that he had succumbed to this illness was no real surprise. Robin Standing, the chief cook, was as careful as any to ensure cleanliness in his kitchen and it's to his credit that outbreaks of food poisoning in the castle were rare. However, hygiene standards in mediaeval kitchens didn't match the conditions in which we expect our food to be prepared today. Added to this, John Howard was lamentably lax in his own personal hygiene, seldom washing his hands, even before eating a meal.

However, being the type of man he was, Baron Howard was determined to find someone else to blame for his recent predicament. The obvious scapegoat was the chief cook, Robin Standing.

In his fury, John Howard declared that Robin had purposely tried to poison him. In those barbaric mediaeval times, the punishment meted out to poisoners was boiling alive. So Robin was paraded before the Baron, informed of his fate and handed over to the custody of Black Giles. The date that this sentence was to be carried out was the following Thursday.

With the exception of Black Giles and a small number of retainers who assisted him as castle gaoler, the whole complement of those who worked in the castle from the youngest page boy to the most senior knight were aghast at the injustice and barbarity of this sentence. Robin Standing was a very popular member of the castle establishment but no one had the courage to make any protest to the Baron. He ruled the castle with a rod of iron and woe betide any who dared to gainsay him.

When Constance met the Lollards at the appointed time at the secret meeting point by the thicket, she brought them up to date with affairs in the castle and reported that the proposed execution would create the diversion needed to carry out their escape plan.

"The whole castle will be paraded into the courtyard to witness this terrible spectacle," she said through the tears of sympathy evoked by the horror of what was about to happen to Robin whom she had really come to like.

While this news of a diversion added to the chance of success of the rescue attempt, the

Lollards were stunned into silence by the magnitude of the evil which was planned for the following Thursday. After some while Matthew spoke and urged them to spend some time in prayer for Robin, that by some means, he would be spared the suffering which was about to be inflicted on him.

After this further time of quiet reflection, Matthew felt able to return to the planned extradition of Thomas de Ros from Pickering.

"One thing further is necessary to make this work. Horses will be needed for Constance and the Baron. We can't risk Constance trying to recover their horses from the castle stable and riding out with the Baron through the main gate. They would certainly be stopped. We must get a message back to Lady Philippa to send an escort and two horses to meet next

Thursday at this rendezvous. Your previous escort to Pickering is obviously aware of its location. Then, next Thursday, Michael and I will separately enter the castle and meet you in the courtyard. It seems that everyone will be there but their attention will be directed elsewhere, and we'll scarcely be noticed."

So it was, on that fateful Thursday, the Lollards met up with Constance at a prearranged place within the castle precinct. They had entered the castle separately, Michael arriving at the castle gate about a quarter of an hour after Matthew. The courtyard was rapidly filling with soldiers and castle workers whom Baron Howard summoned to witness the barbaric execution.

"The sooner we get this done the better," suggested Matthew. "If you go now to where your horses and escort have been arranged to wait outside the castle, Michael will go to Thomas de Ros's cell. All going well, I'll leave the castle first. Thomas de Ros in Lollard garb will leave a few minutes later and after a further interval, Michael will follow us out."

Constance and Michael nodded assent. Although the plan seemed a good one, they were filled with trepidation. Some unforeseen event could scupper the whole exercise with disastrous consequences.

Constance made her way out of the main castle gate. The guards were familiar with her going to and fro from the castle but today, they were paying more attention to what was going on within the courtyard than checking the identity of those leaving the castle. This would work in favour of the planned escape. There was a heart-stopping moment as Michael went to enter the tower from which he could access Thomas de

Ros's prison cell, when a soldier challenged him, asking him where he was going. As a result of his missionary work among the occupants of the castle during his recent visits, Michael knew the names of several who lived and worked in the castle.

"Mistress Stackpole has asked me to meet her here," he bluffed.

The name was obviously known to the soldier.

"More than likely, she's already in the courtyard," the soldier replied, "but if not she's more likely to be found in the keep than in this tower."

"No," insisted Michael, "She definitely said that she would be here."

The soldier just nodded and moved on to another part of the courtyard.

Michael breathed again. He entered the tower, mounted the spiral staircase until he came to the door which opened on to the defensive wall, made his way to the prison tower and down the spiral stairway to the room where Thomas de Ros was imprisoned. He slid back the bolts, opened the door and put his fingers to his lips to indicate to the astonished looking Baron that silence was important. In a quiet voice, Michael explained the plan to Thomas, indicated that he should shave and dress in the habit which Matthew was carrying in his bag and then they could make their way out. Thomas was ready within minutes and they cautiously left the cell, closing and bolting the door behind them. They made their way back along the route that Michael had used to reach Baron Thomas and descended to the courtyard. Following the plan that had been explained to him, the Thomas made his way alone to the main gate. He was not challenged as he left. The guards had seen two Lollards enter earlier that morning but they were still paying more attention to what was going on in the courtyard than noting the identity of persons leaving the castle. Thomas made his way to the prearranged rendezvous where Matthew and Constance were waiting with the horses and two soldiers who would escort them back to Helmsley. Ten minutes later, Michael left the castle. The guards seemed unaware that although two religieux had been seen to enter the castle, three were leaving! Michael, carrying the bag with the Thomas's real clothes, arrived at the prearranged rendezvous. Thomas changed back into his own clothes and a few minutes later, Constance and de Ros were ready to set off. They stayed briefly to express a sincere and heartfelt word of thanks to the Lollards who had planned this escape. Matthew and Michael returned to Pickering to continue their missionary work in the town. Over the next couple of days, they planned to revisit the castle a few times. They thought that if they disappeared from the scene at the same time as the Baron and Constance, it would provide a clue as to how the escape had been planned.

On their next visit to the castle the buzz was very much about what had happened at the planned execution. Things had not gone according to Baron Howard's plans. The courtyard of the castle had filled with soldiers from the castle garrison and members of the castle workforce. They watched in silence as Black Giles' men built a mound of wooden logs and surmounted this with a giant cauldron. Baron John Howard was observing proceedings from a window in the castle keep overlooking the courtyard. The cauldron was filled by buckets of water conveyed by a bucket chain manned by Black Giles' men. Then, Robin Standing was brought out, his arms bound tightly to his sides. When besides the log pile, he was forced to his knees and Giles men bent him double and tied the upper part of his legs to his body so that his knees were just beneath his chin and there would be no possibility of his standing up once consigned to the cauldron. It took all four of Giles' men to lift him to the top of the log pile and dump him in the cauldron. Now was the time for Giles himself to light the flames. He'd been ordered by Baron Howard to maintain the temperature of the cauldron at a temperature which would keep Robin screaming for at least an hour before he finally died. However, this was not to happen.

A whoosh was heard as an arrow was dispatched from high up in one of the towers. This struck Robin, possibly killing him outright. Then followed a cascade of arrows fired from arrow slits in towers all round the courtyard, some just hitting the cauldron but most finding their mark and hitting Robin from all directions. If the first arrow hadn't killed him, the subsequent volley certainly did. Soldiers of the castle garrison had determined that if they hadn't the courage to mutiny, they would at least save Robin from suffering the dreadful death planned for him.

Giles looked around, his face even more contorted in anger than usual. The same was probably the case with Baron Howard but he couldn't be seen as he must have immediately vacated his lofty vantage point. Who had fired these arrows? Nothing could be seen moving behind the many arrow slits from which the volley of arrows had been fired. The courtyard was in pandemonium. The archers would have been able to join the confused melee in the courtyard without any chance of their being detected as being involved in loosing the arrows which had prevented Robin from being boiled alive. There was mixed feeling among the complement of castle workers and soldiers, sadness that a popular fellow worker had been killed but relief that he had been spared terrible suffering.

Black Giles made his way to the keep, no doubt to confer with Baron Howard. While absolutely furious that their plans for Robin Standing's execution had been thwarted by their own people, they also experienced the frustration of knowing that there was no way they could find out which individuals had been responsible for this affront to their authority. This anger and frustration was increased tenfold when they discovered that Baron Thomas de Ros and Constance had escaped the castle. There was no way Baron Howard could apportion blame to

Black Giles because he had been relieved for a time of his duties as gaoler to carry out Baron Howard's planned atrocity.

A few days later, Matthew and Michael returned to Helmsley to find Baron and Lady de Ros preparing to leave.

"As known Lancastrian supporters, we no longer feel safe, remaining in our own castle," explained Thomas de Ros. "The castle is secure enough, I would say impregnable, against all but the most determined and resourceful of foes but Baron Howard won't have taken kindly to knowing he has been tricked. He won't attempt an assault on the castle but he'll send spies to keep watch on my movements to discover when there might be opportunities to capture me again, should I venture out of the castle We have decided that our place is with Henry and Margaret. News has it that they escaped to Scotland after Towton but they're now raising forces among their allies in Wales. While we're away, our son, Edmund, will nominally be in charge of the castle, but of course, as he's not yet ten, he can't really be burdened with this responsibility and the one who'll really be in charge is my steward, Joseph."

During the time they had spent with the de Ros's in Helmsley Castle, the Lollards had become well acquainted with both Edmund, a really sensible boy, and Joseph, whom they had found to be not only responsible but very intelligent and highly educated for one in service.

Matthew and Michael related what had happened at Pickering Castle after their escape. While being extremely sad that a good man like Robin Standing should be dead, they were glad that the manner of his death had been more humane than the atrocity planned by Baron John Howard.

A few days later, the de Ros's left for Wales. They were travelling with five men at arms from the castle garrison, and Philippa was accompanied by three ladies in waiting, including Constance.

Chapter 11

The Orphanage

Matthew and Michael continued their work in the villages around Helmsley. This work was both evangelical and pastoral.

One day when it had been raining hard, they were distressed to discover a thin little boy shivering in wet clothing.

"Why aren't you at home indoors on a day like this?" inquired Matthew.

"I don't have a proper home," he mournfully replied. "My mother died and my father was killed in the war. I sleep in a shed next to my aunty's house. She lives there with my uncle, their five children and my other aunty. They're so crowded that there's no room for me in the house as well."

The boy gave his name as Jacob. The Lollards went to visit his aunt's house. It was as he had described it. Judith, the boy's aunt was a kindly woman. She lamented the fact that her house was so crowded that she couldn't provide Jacob with adequate accommodation. She assured the Lollards however that he was as well fed as her other children and as her means allowed. Judith then cited a number of other children who were in the same straights as Jacob as a result of the wars.

Matthew and Michael discussed the problem as they sadly trudged back to the castle.

Something must be done," said Matthew. "We can't solve the problem by ourselves but we can give some leadership as we did before to solve the problem of shortage of manpower on the estates. With Lord and Lady de Ros away, we'll have to consult with de Ros's steward, Joseph, to find a way to deal with this."

The meeting with Joseph was constructive. Edmund de Ros was present. Although too young to contribute to the discussion, he was old enough to understand what was going on and was very attentive. The Lollards considered that the boy was getting a good education in practical Christianity which was important for one who was going to succeed to an aristocratic title and the responsibility that went with it.

"Last time a problem affecting the community came up, it was dealt with by holding a meeting of members of the local communities. I think that we could do the same again," advised Joseph.

"I agree," said Michael, "but I think the onus is on us to first come up with an outline plan. The locals, who have a more detailed knowledge of their society, might reject our plan. If so, they will be challenged to come up with a better plan or suggest amendments to any plan we put forward."

"We must make it clear that meeting the interests of these destitute children is our prime objective." added Matthew. "The problem is fairly simple to state. Orphaned children are living on the Helmsley estates with inadequate shelter and food."

"That's clear enough," said Joseph. "The way I see it is that the community must work collectively to construct a building which will function as an orphanage but the building alone is not enough. It'll need to be adequately furnished and most important of all, it must be supervised by adults prepared to sacrificially love these children."

"Well said," "Absolutely," the Lollards responded.

"So who then should we invite to this meeting?" queried Matthew. "The last meeting held to deal with a local issue was successful but it made slow headway because too many people were present."

"I would suggest the leaders of the various farm collectives which were set up should provide adequate representation," advised Michael.

So it was that another meeting was convened in the great hall of the castle keep. Some twenty leading men were present. Memories of the way the last crisis had been dealt with were still fresh in everybody's mind and the wisdom the Lollards had demonstrated in resolving the problem was generally appreciated and afforded them considerable credibility. There was complete agreement that this was also a problem which had to be dealt with but, initially, they were less ready to accept the plan outlined by Joseph and the Lollards.

"Although everybody is now a member of a collective farm community so that no one is destitute, we're still short of manpower," explained one of the collective farm leaders. "We had to work to the limits to prepare fields which hadn't been properly ploughed in the autumn to get them ready for late planting of seed which we are hoping will germinate and produce a good crop. We just don't have the capacity to release manpower to construct the building you are suggesting."

Some murmured assent to this comment. However, most of those present remained in thoughtful silence, agreeing with the sentiments just expressed but knowing they couldn't walk away from the problem which had been presented. A more positive voice spoke up.

"You're quite wrong to say that no-one is destitute. The very reason we're meeting is that these kids are destitute. What hope have these poor orphans? It's our responsibility not just to see them survive but give them some prospect of a future when they'll be able to contribute to our community."

A rather more enthusiastic assent was murmured to this contribution to the discussion.

Another spoke in support of his colleague.

"James is quite right. Yes, we have been pushed to our limits over the past weeks but now summer is upon us, things are getting easier. The women are really pulling their weight in helping with so many of the manual jobs which were previously only done by men. Can't each of us provide one worker to be involved in this project for just two days each week? I estimate that this would provide six people every day."

There was further murmuring as those present discussed this among themselves. Joseph added that additional labour would be provided by some of the men garrisoning the castle provided there was no military threat from outside.

After a few moments, James who seemed to be accepted as the spokesman for the group addressed Joseph and the Lollards.

"Everyone present now seems to be in agreement with your suggestion in principle but there are many details which need to be sorted out first. How many children need to be catered for?

Who'll supervise them when they're living there? How will they be fed?"

"Well said," responded Matthew, "Let's consider your first question. This is one you can answer. You're the people who represent the community. You must know how many destitute children are running around."

The group then broke up into further murmured discussion. After a while James spoke up again.

"There may be more but we've come up with the names of five boys and three girls who are living rough."

Joseph, who seemed to have some knowledge of building, then spoke up.

"This is a good starting point from which to make plans. I'd been thinking about what the building might look like before this meeting was convened. At each end, there'll need to be dormitories, one for the boys and another for the girls. The main living quarters will need to be between the dormitories and must include washing space, a cooking area and a general living space where the children can eat their meals and do the things kids do when not playing outside. It'll also be up to our communities to provide the furniture, beds, chairs and tables. However, there's no point in starting this project if we can't identify people from among our community who'd be 'de facto' full time parents for these kids and live in the orphanage with them."

The gathered company was now beginning to get enthusiastically excited, now a vision of the details of something important was being shared. They realised that it would be a challenge but it was achievable. They started to discuss things among themselves and after a while, James spoke for them again.

"Three of us have widowed sisters or sisters-in-law living in overcrowded conditions in our own homes and there'll be other young widows around in a similar predicament. We know that several of these would just love the opportunity of becoming house mothers should this project take off."

"One further decision to be made," added Joseph, practical as ever. "We need to identify the site where this orphanage is to be built."

More murmuring and discussion. Finally, James spoke up again.

"There's a stretch of scrubland by the mill. It's no use to anybody, or hasn't been until now. It'll need clearing but that won't take too long. It's flat so no levelling is going to be needed. Let's go with that."

"All right," said Joseph. "I'll draw up some plans. If these seem satisfactory to everybody here, we could get going within the month if not the week."

Michael concluded the meeting.

"I think we've covered everything that needs to be considered for the time being. Thank you all for coming and contributing in such a positive spirit. We can now draw this meeting to a close and arrange to meet again at a later date when further decisions will need to be made."

Those present got up and made their way out, talking excitedly to one another. Matthew and Michael realised that a communal project like this would really draw the community together. There was a generally 'feel good' atmosphere as everybody departed.

As they reviewed what had taken place that morning, Matthew and Michael realised that it was remiss of them not to have included the Vicar in the deliberations and they decided to put him in the picture at the next available opportunity. When they met up with the Reverend Will Hakford, he was full of praise for what the Lollards had achieved.

"I have one further suggestion to make," he said. "In this day and age, it's going to be very important that people should be able to read and write. The future is going to require a literate population. Arrangements need to be made to educate the children in the orphanage. There's no proper school in Helmsley. Indeed, if we can find suitable teachers and the main living room in the orphanage is large enough to double up as a schoolroom, other children living in the nearby homes could also be invited to join the orphanage children for lessons."

The Lollards enthusiastically agreed. However, the same sort of challenge existed as had been encountered in the discussion with community leaders which had led to the setting up of collective farms. There was then a shortage of manpower and in this case, fairly educated manpower was needed. How would such a school be staffed? Teaching was a specialist job which few in that community were qualified to carry out. The Vicar volunteered his services.

"I can't pretend that my job here keeps me so busy that I couldn't find the time to spend one or two half days at the school. I'm sure that Edmund's tutor in the castle could be recruited to help and you yourselves are more than well-educated enough to teach and contribute to this work."

Yes, this was a good suggestion but the Lollards pointed out that their vocation required that they should not be located in one place too long and the time would soon be coming when they would have to move on. However, Matthew and Michael were fully agreeable to being involved in teaching at the outset of the school being set up. They'd see how plans materialised from there.

A fortnight later, under James leadership and with guidance from Joseph, the site for the new orphanage was being cleared and the wood and other materials needed for the building were being assembled.

Chapter 12

The Turncoats

As the Battle of Towton turned in the Yorkists failure, the Duke of Somerset had been no longer able to rally his troops who were being routed and fleeing from the battlefield. Seeing that all was lost, Somerset realised that he would have to warn Henry and Elizabeth and enable them to escape the pursuing Yorkists.

Somerset met up with King Henry, Queen Margaret and Prince Edward in the Clifford Tower, York's main castle, and briefly recounted the sad tale of the battle, emphasising the decisive factor the weather had been in causing the inevitable outcome.

They couldn't afford to wait. The Yorkists would be hot on their heels. They considered travelling by a route which avoided main roads but abandoned this idea as speed was of the essence and they needed to get as far north as possible before nightfall. It was getting quite dark by the time they reached Thirsk and they put up in an inn, the innkeeper having no idea that this was a royal party. The news of Towton was yet to reach that far north. At break of day they continued northwards, breaking their journey at Alnwick and Bamburgh, castles held by the Earl of Northumberland, a Lancastrian ally, finally reaching Berwick two days later. Once in Scotland, the immediate danger was past and they could proceed with less haste to Edinburgh where they were welcomed by King James III. His father, James II, had died the previous year and Margaret's friend, Mary of Gueldres, was now dowager queen.

Some time later, they were joined by Thomas and Philippa de Ros and their small entourage which included Constance. Thomas de Ros was specially glad to become reacquainted with Edward of Westminster, Prince of Wales, as he had been knighted by Edward after the second battle of St. Albans. Queen Margaret had arrived in Scotland without any attendants. She soon became impressed with Constance and asked Lady Philippa de Ros if she could take Constance into her own service. Philippa had arrived in Scotland with three ladies in waiting and was only too pleased to be able provide support for the Queen in this way although sorry that of all her ladies, Constance was the one who had caught the Queen's eye.

There wasn't another Scottish army available for Margaret to launch a counter attack against Edward but the Duke of Somerset set about raising troops. After a year or so, when he thought that he had enough men, Somerset, together with King Henry and Baron de Ros entered England. Somerset's army was defeated at the Battle of Hedgeley Moor in April and suffered a final defeat a month later at the Battle of Hexham. Somerset and de Ros were captured and executed. This was a great loss to the Lancastrian cause. Somerset and de Ros had been conspicuous in their bravery and loyal service to King Henry and Queen Margaret.

King Henry escaped and managed to find refuge in the houses of Lancastrian supporters in the north of England. However, he was being hotly sought after by the Yorkists and could never stay in one place for long. A year later, he was made welcome by Sir Richard Tempest at his home, Waddington Hall, in Lancashire. Sadly for Henry, this didn't prove a safe refuge. Although Sir Richard was loyal, his brother, John, wasn't and

John tipped off someone who is only known as a black monk of Addington. He informed the Yorkists of Henry's whereabouts, probably in hope of a financial reward, and they came to search Waddington Hall. An escape plan had been put in place for Henry and he fled into nearby woods, hiding up in the undergrowth at a place called Brungerley Hippings. This was near a place where the River Ribble could be crossed by stepping stones. Henry's hiding place was not secure. He was discovered, captured and sent to London where he was held in the Tower.

Meanwhile, King Edward came to terms with James III of Scotland. England had not been favourably disposed towards the Scots since they allied with France during the Hundred Years' War. However, this was now well in the past and Queen Margaret realised that Scotland was no longer a safe country of refuge. She made her way to France with her son, Edward of Westminster.

Although King Edward now felt well established on the English throne, problems were brewing at court. Warwick and his family were spending quite a bit of time in the company of King Edward's family. Edward's brothers, George,

Duke of Clarence, and Richard, Duke of Gloucester, fell in love with the Earl of Warwick's daughters, Isabel and Anne. They were both very attractive girls. Isabel was attracted by George's carefree personality, quite a contrast to the intensity of her ambitious father. Anne on the other hand admired the steadfast loyalty that Richard displayed towards his brother, Edward. During the recent conflicts, she had seen that loyalty was in short supply as battles had turned on lords leading their followings to change sides, even within the heat of battle. She was about to experience another act of disloyalty. In spite of the protests of his brothers, the King refused to give permission for George and Richard to marry the Earl of Warwick's daughters, matches which the Earl of Warwick favoured.

The Earl of Warwick was in France, attempting to arrange a prestigious marriage for King Edward and he returned, satisfied that he could offer Edward the choice of two eminently suitable brides, King Louis XI's daughter, Anne, or his sister-in-law, Bona of Savoy. Louis XI was the son of Charles VII under whom the English had been expelled from France, so ending the

Hundred Years' War and Henry's claim to the French throne by virtue of his descent from Charles VII's father, and his sister, Catherine of Valois.

Warwick was absolutely furious when he returned and was told that Edward had married in secret Elizabeth Woodville, daughter of an obscure knight who had supported the Lancastrian cause. Elizabeth may have been a beautiful woman but she was already a widow and in Warwick's opinion, of insufficient noble rank to make her a fit wife for a king, especially as he had negotiated the prospect of much better marriages for the king at no small expense to Warwick's patience and negotiating skills. Things started to get worse for Warwick who had previously been Edward's prime confidant and most ardent supporter. Warwick found himself being sidelined, his place being taken by lowborn relatives of this upstart strumpet, Elizabeth Woodville.

One day as Warwick and Clarence met, they started to air their grievances.

"What right has Edward to obstruct the plans of Isabel and myself to get married?" complained Clarence. "Anyone would be proud to marry your daughters, Warwick. I'm surprised that Edward didn't pull rank and marry Isabel himself but there he is, going ahead with marrying just about the most unsuitable person you could imagine."

As their discussions continued, Warwick had the temerity to suggest that perhaps the time had come when Edward should be removed from the throne. Warwick gave more than a hint to Clarence that he could then become king in his brother's place.

"I put him on the throne," Warwick contemptuously boasted, "and I can just as easily remove him"

So it was, Warwick and Clarence changed sides. Clarence went ahead and married Warwick's daughter, Isabel. Warwick and Clarence then engaged and defeated King Edward in battle at Edgecote Moor and imprisoned Edward in Middleham Castle. With King Henry imprisoned in the Tower of London, the nation was in the strange position of having both contenders for the throne, held separately in prison by the Earl of Warwick.

Chapter 13

Enemies Reconciled

There was little support for Warwick or Clarence in the country while King Edward was in prison. Within months, Edward was released from prison by his supporters and he set about raising the forces which would restore him to power. Warwick and Clarence instigated a revolt against Edward but by then, Edward had raised sufficient troops to put down this revolt at the Battle of Losecoat Field. Warwick and Clarence were declared traitors. Realising that the tables had turned against them, they fled to France where Queen Margaret had taken refuge with her son, Prince Edward. King Louis XI suggested that Warwick and Margaret should join forces in order to recover Henry's throne in England. Louis needed to create an alliance which could forestall any attempt by the Duke of Burgundy to form a hostile alliance against him with King Edward. At first, Margaret vehemently disagreed with any suggestion that she and Warwick should form an alliance. She was almost as hostile to the Earl of Warwick as she had been to the Duke of York at the beginning of the Roses War. They were sworn enemies. However, both Margaret and Warwick were forced to be pragmatic. Separately, they could never recover their power in England. By combining their forces, they just might.

The initial meeting between Warwick and Margaret to achieve this truce was very strained. Proud Margaret had insisted that Warwick knelt before her to indicate that he had respect for her rank. It must have pained him to do this but if this was necessary to achieve the required reconciliation, he was prepared to do just that. This thawed the atmosphere and negotiations proceeded well from that point. Warwick and Margaret's forces would land in England and move into London where Henry would be released from the Tower and restored to the throne. To cement this alliance, it was agreed that Edward, the young Prince of Wales, should marry Warwick's younger daughter, Anne.

When she was informed of this arrangement, Anne was not pleased and protested against this marriage being arranged for her.

"But I love Richard of Gloucester," she insisted, "and he's the one I want to marry."

Warwick persuaded her as gently as possible that marriage to Richard was now out of the question and her marriage to Prince Edward would put her in line to become the next Queen of England. Anne at last reluctantly agreed to the match. Clarence on the other hand viewed this arrangement with suspicion. Was Warwick hedging his bets on who might become the next King of England after Edward was deposed and Henry restored?

Warwick returned to England, landing at Dartmouth. He gained support as he marched to London through the southern counties and released King Henry from the Tower. He paraded with the restored King through London. Thus, the Earl of Warwick who had previously helped Edward win the throne became known as Kingmaker. Warwick was joined by his brother, John Neville, who brought a significant force with him from the Scottish marches.

King Edward was in the north, dealing with an uprising in Yorkshire and was unprepared for Warwick's return. He and his brother, Richard, Duke of Gloucester, left Doncaster and crossed the channel to Bruges. Edward's brother in law, the Duke of Burgundy, provided Edward with troops and he returned to England, landing at Ravenspur on the Yorkshire coast. His brother, Clarence, changed sides again and joined Edward as he marched to London. Having captured London and confining King Henry to the Tower again, he moved to Barnet, just north of London to engage Warwick's army encamped on the top of the hill. Like the Battle of Towton, the outcome of this battle was again influenced by weather conditions. Edward's army maintained silence as they approached Barnet in a thick fog and unbeknown to Warwick's troops, camped just below the hill where the Earl's army was encamped. Just before the break of day the following morning, Edward's army crept up the hill, still shrouded in fog, and attacked Warwick's camp before his army was even awake. In the confusion which reigned, Warwick's troops even started fighting among themselves. The Earl of Warwick was killed in the battle. Edward's victory was absolute.

Margaret and Prince Edward had landed in the West Country a few days before the Battle of Barnet and now they could no longer link with

Warwick's troops so a change of plan was needed. Margaret decided to march to Wales to pick up reinforcements from her Lancastrian supporters in the Principality but was thwarted when she reached the only suitable crossing point at the city of Gloucester where she was refused passage. She headed back into England where she met Edward's forces at Tewkesbury. In spite of her rousing speech to rally her troops, Edward's forces defeated her smaller army. Margaret's soldiers fled into the town, many of them seeking sanctuary in Tewkesbury Abbey. The pursuing Yorkist troops paid no heed to the laws of sanctuary and massacred the soldiers they caught including those in the Abbey. Edward, Prince of Wales, was among those killed in the fighting. Margaret was captured. She was first confined in Wallingford Castle but soon transferred to the more secure Tower of London where her husband, Henry, was already held prisoner. The loss of the battle and the death of the son on whom her hopes had rested had completely broken Margaret's spirit. She was no longer the forceful and even aggressive woman who had been the power behind the throne during Henry's troubled reign.

Henry and Margaret were confined separately in the Tower of London, Henry in the Wakefield Tower and Margaret in the more comfortable quarters in St. Thomas's Tower, located above the water gate which allowed direct entry into the Tower from the River Thames. Later, this entry became known as 'Traitors' Gate', the safest way to conduct political prisoners to the Tower. Entry by this gate avoided the possibility of the prisoner being rescued by their supporters on the congested streets of London. Margaret was placed in the custody of a former lady in waiting, Alice Chaucer, Duchess of Suffolk. She was allowed to retain Constance as a companion and lady in waiting.

Chapter 14

The Tower

Dark, disturbing thoughts were passing through the mind of King Edward.

"My popularity is waning. The defection of Warwick and Clarence to Henry has been a wake-up call. While Henry is still alive, restoring him to the throne would be a focus and excuse for any rebellious baron who wants to revolt and rise in arms against me. I can't trust Clarence and even though Gloucester seems loyal enough, who really knows what thoughts are passing through his head. Henry must be eliminated, but how? He can't be put on trial and judicially murdered. Ineffective as a king he may have been, but he has done nothing morally wrong. On the contrary, he's a model of saintliness and everyone knows this. I must resort to other means to get him out of the way."

Edward's thoughts then shifted to speculate whether there was anyone who might perform a dirty deed for him. One name came up.

"John Howard owes me a favour. I knighted him after the Battle of Towton and he's been awarded other honours since. It's well known that he has a servant who delights in carrying out executions and assassinations."

So it was that John Howard was summoned to meet with the King at the Tower of London, bringing his steward, Giles Noirmont (Black Giles), along with him. They met in the house by Tower Green occupied by the Constable, John Sutton, Baron Dudley. They believed that they were meeting in secret but an event like the visit of the King aroused curiosity and needless to say, someone eavesdropped the deliberations taking place in the Constable's house.

A date was set for the deed to be done. Black Giles was to arrive late at night at the Tower and be given free passage into the Tower by the guards on duty. He would then make his way to the Wakefield Tower where he would find a key in the lock of the room where Henry was confined. Having carried out the required assassination, he would leave the Tower promptly by the way he came in and payment would be made to him via John Howard.

News was around the Tower before the Constable had even taken King Edward, John Howard and Black Giles to reconnoitre the Tower and identify the Wakefield Tower where Henry was held. This would be fairly easy to identify, even at night, being directly opposite St. Thomas's Tower, Queen Margaret's prison. This was conspicuous as being the tower directly above gate which allowed access to the Tower of London from the river. Dark deeds like the one being planned had been executed before in the Tower and would be again. Everybody who lived or worked in the Tower knew about them but there was a code by which such matters were never disclosed beyond the Tower precincts.

Unlike Margaret, Constance, her lady-in-waiting was not restricted to remain in St. Thomas's Tower. Although serving the Queen, she was not a prisoner but a free woman at liberty to move around the Tower when not required by her mistress. As we know, Constance was a very personable young woman and made friends with many of those who served in the Tower. Constance came to know of the evil plan afoot from Agnes, one of the Tower kitchen maids. Constance was appalled but what could she do.

She confided in Alice Chaucer, the Queen's custodian. She discovered that the Duchess Alice had independently heard this rumour but like Constance, there appeared to be nothing she could do. Her responsibility was restricted to supervising the Queen and her needs. This involved a daily constitutional walk round the Tower grounds but otherwise, the Queen was confined to her prison. The Duchess and Constance felt it prudent not to share this information with the Queen and avoid causing her further unnecessary stress but their minds were continuously engaged in searching for some way in which the King might be spared the fate planned for him.

Meanwhile, what was happening in Helmsley?. Lady Philippa de Ros had long since returned from Wales where she had said farewell to her husband, not knowing then that she would never see him again. Constance, whose service had been transferred to the Queen, was now, no longer with Lady de Ros.

Lady Philippa had been heartbroken on hearing of the death of her brave husband. After a few days of inconsolable grief, she realised that she had to get her life back under control. This is what Thomas would have expected of her. She felt proud that Thomas had died in the service of his King and Queen. She was proud to see that young Edmund was growing in stature and responsibility. Yes, Thomas would live on through Edmund and it was up to her to do the very best she could to ensure that as Edmund entered his majority, he would continue to live in the noble tradition set by his father.

Lady Philippa thoroughly approved the construction of the orphanage which had been the brainchild of the Lollards. Construction was nearly complete. Beds had been made and installed and already, the orphans were able to sleep in warm and dry conditions. There was still more work to be done in constructing furniture, tables and chairs, so that the children could eat in the orphanage and receive lessons. For the time being, they were still having to return to their overcrowded former foster homes to be fed. Although Matthew and Michael had made the castle their base, they were often away for days at a time, sometimes longer, carrying out their missionary work.

Lady Philippa was able to keep up to date with the progress of the war through the news that messengers brought to Helmsley from the action spots where the course of history was being settled. She was aware of the outcome of the Battle of Tewkesbury and knew that Constance was living in the Tower of London as lady-in-waiting to the imprisoned Queen. She felt an overwhelming urge to make contact with Constance to let her know how life was progressing at Helmsley and to inform her, if she didn't already know, of the death of Baron Thomas. She knew that the most secure way of sending a letter to Constance was to use the Lollards to deliver this, should they be prepared to conduct their missionary activities as far afield as London. When they returned from their most recent missionary foray, she asked them if they would be kind enough to carry out this errand. Matthew and Michael welcomed this as an opportunity to meet up with Constance again and a few days later they set off for London.

After several days, preaching at the towns and villages through which they passed on their journey, they arrived in London. They'd never been there before and while being impressed on the one hand by the magnificent buildings and churches, they were certainly unimpressed by the sorry sanitary conditions in this overcrowded city. Waterways like the River Fleet ran as open sewers, discharging unsanitary waste into the Thames. However, they did enjoy the atmosphere created by the mellow chimes of the mediaeval church bells summoning the faithful to worship and adding to the rather special ambience of the city.

As religieux, they had no difficulty in being given access to the Tower, especially when they let it be known that they were bearing an important letter for Constance, the former Queen's lady-in-waiting. Constance was already a firm favourite with the garrison of the Tower which included those on guard at the entrances. After undergoing the formality of being searched for concealed weapons, they were ushered through the Lion's Tower, the Middle Tower and the Byward Tower. St. Thomas's Tower was then just a short distance on the right as they entered the main Tower precincts. Here, they experienced a joyful reunion with Constance. They'd arrived the day following Constance's discovery that in a few days' time, an attempt would be made to assassinate Henry.

After whispering this information to the Lollards, the three of them moved on to Tower Green where they could sit near the site where the scaffold was set up when executions were arranged. They could sit here and talk quietly without any chance of their being overheard.

Constance was delighted to receive the letter from Lady Philippa. Yes, she did know that Thomas de Ros had been killed. Thomas and Philippa had been to Constance the ones she had loved and respected, more than anyone could have realised. They had become her adoptive parents since they had taken her into their care when she had become an orphan. For many days, Constance had periods when she was unable to control the flow of her tears as she remembered Thomas and all he had been to her. She remembered how she'd been able to save his life, after the Battle of Towton with the help of her Lollard friends, Matthew and Michael. This memory was of some comfort to her. Her grief was tempered by the delight of knowing how well young Edmund was growing up and filling his father's role at Helmsley Castle. Having been orphaned herself, Constance was fascinated to hear about the orphanage which had been built and was now, almost fully furnished. The Lollards could also bring Constance up to date on other members of the castle establishment at Helmsley whom she would have known well. Now came the serious part of the discussion. The Lollards asked for time to think through the implications of what she had told them.

Matthew spoke first. Dangerous as was the action he was about to suggest, he knew that Michael would go along with him.

"As it seems that only one person has been briefed to carry out this dastardly deed, the two of us could wait inside the King's cell and defend him from being murdered. Yes, this would involve killing the would-be assassin and that's normally against our code but we would feel fully justify doing this if that's what's needed to save someone from being brutally murdered, especially if he was the King."

Michael made a minor correction to Matthew's statement.

"We'd be fully prepared to adopt this extreme course of action, so totally opposed to our code, whether or not the intended murder victim was the King."

Matthew nodded in assent to this correction and then returned to the practicalities of the situation.

"To protect the King, we'd have to be in the Tower at night when the murder is scheduled to take place and have some means of concealing the King, or better still, getting him out of the Tower."

"Yes," replied Constance, "if we can get the King out of the Tower before Black Giles comes to set about his evil business, that would be fine but the castle guard patrols are fairly frequent during daylight hours and if Black Giles enters the King's cell and finds him gone, he'll raise the alarm that the King has escaped. Then there'll be a hue and cry until he's recaptured and it's unlikely that you'll be far enough from the Tower to be safe. We know that Black Giles will wait until dark before he sets about assassinating the King but we just don't know the actual time he's planned to do this deed."

This challenge facing them seemed immense and the three remained in silence for a while, praying as they contemplated any other options open.

Constance spoke next.

"The Queen is imprisoned in the Tower above the water gate where you met me. This gate allows access to the Tower from the river and is not guarded. It's quite easy to open, using one of the small boats which is permanently moored in the pool this side of the gate. If you could hire a small boat from somewhere on the Thames near the Tower, I could enable you enter the Tower by this route. If you are then successful in killing Black Giles to protect the King, the three of you could make your escape in this boat. I would fasten the gate behind you. It wouldn't be until the following morning that they will discover that Black Giles is dead and the King has gone."

They were now beginning to get quite animated in their discussion as the plan unfolded.

"We can do even better than that," added Matthew. "If, as you tell us, Black Giles from Pickering is to be the assassin, we know that he's bearded while Henry's always clean shaven. If we kill Black Giles, shave him and get the King to change clothes with him, we can leave the body of Black Giles as if he were the dead King and escape with the real King. Those who are sent to deal with the King's corpse probably don't know what he looks like anyway. It will be assumed that the assassination had gone to plan, Black Giles had left the building and would return to Baron John Howard to collect his reward."

Constance and Michael gave an excited clap at this plan. It seemed a good idea but the question remained as to whether they really could kill Black Giles before he carried out his evil deed. There was one outstanding problem to be solved.

"Being religieux, we possess no money or weapons," said Michael. "We'll need both to perform this deed, money to hire a boat and knives to deny Black Giles access to his intended victim."

"I can provide both," volunteered Constance. "I'll give you the money you need as you leave here now and I'll have suitable knives from the kitchen available when you come on Thursday, the day scheduled for this murder."

They made their way back to St. Thomas's Tower where Constance disappeared briefly to return a few moments later with more than sufficient money to hire a small boat. They bade farewell to Constance and the three of then separated, all in a state of excitement at the dangerous task which lay before them but not without experiencing some trepidation.

Knowing that Lady Alice Chaucer was aware of the attempt which was going to be made on the King's life, Constance confided in her the plans for Thursday night. Also, as the Queen's custodian, she would need to know why Constance, her lady-in-waiting, had to leave St. Thomas's Tower in the night. Lady Alice was very impressed with the plan. She had one further thing she would like to be included in the arrangements.

"The Queen would dearly like to be able to meet up with Henry, even if only for a short period," she said. "If things go well, according to plan, could the King come up and spend just an hour with the Queen before he makes his escape? It's been so frustrating for the Queen to know that Henry is no more than a stone's throw away and not even be able to see him. I know there are things she'll want to unburden herself over and she desperately wants to do this. She feels full of guilt, that it's been her overbearing and aggressive attitude and actions which have brought them to the sorry state in which they now find themselves."

Provided the rescue went as planned, there was no reason why this meeting shouldn't take place.

Now came the practical preparation which would need to be put in hand by the time the Lollards came to fulfil their dangerous role in this venture. How would Constance get the knives? She couldn't just walk into the kitchen, pick them up and walk out under the cook's nose. Constance already had a plan in mind. She was an observant young woman. She knew that every day, the scullion's job was to sharpen the kitchen knives. As a large number of individuals garrisoning the Tower had to be fed, a correspondingly large number of knives had to be used in food preparation. The scullion didn't sharpen the knives in the kitchen but each day, he took them out with his whetstone to a quiet spot behind the kitchen where he would be out of sight. This gave him the opportunity of scooting off to spend time with his sweetheart, Constance's friend, the kitchen maid, Agnes, when she had her break. He would leave the knives in his secret spot but unguarded. Constance waited her opportunity, watching for the lovers to go off on their tryst. Once the coast was clear, Constance nipped into the scullion's hidey hole. What an array of knives she discovered, carving knives, many smaller knives for the preparation of vegetables, and all manner of table knives. Constance quickly assessed which knives would be suitable for the job in hand, stowed them in her bag and made a quick exit. They wouldn't be missed from such a large assortment of cutlery.

Meanwhile, Lady Alice brought her mind to focus on the plan afoot. In her position, she had to be specially careful. For her, the consequences of being found to be involved in an attempt to rescue King Henry could be fatal. She asked herself, what would be the appearance of the Lollards and the King on leaving the Wakefield Tower if they'd been successful in dispatching Black

Giles? A bloody mess. Questions would be asked if they were seen wandering about London in that state and they certainly would need to avoid drawing attention to themselves. Being a duchess, she was the most socially elevated person in the Tower, outranking even the Constable who was a mere baron. She was therefore held in considerable deference by all the occupants of the Tower as she moved around on her regular constitutional sorties and people were always ready to do her favours, especially as she related to them with a great deal of natural charm.

She first went to the laundry where clothes which were past their best were regularly discarded and asked if she could have any spare unwanted garments which she could use for a sewing project which she had started. She was given her pick and soon found some doublets and hose which would serve her purpose well. Her eye was taken by a fairly splendid tabard which she thought would be suitable for the King but immediately changed her mind. The King shouldn't leave the Tower wearing anything which would make him conspicuous in any way. She put the garments she had chosen in her bag.

Her next port of call was the armoury. The Lollards were not experienced fighters. They had never been involved in an act of violence in their lives. Even two of them may not be a match for Black Giles who had no doubt carried out a number of killings in his life. She knew the armourer would not allow swords out of his armoury but he would let her have a couple of shields if she could provide a good cover story. She asked the armourer if she could look around at some of the shields. Two small ones caught her eye as being ideal to provide the sort of protection the Lollards might need.

"I'm in the process of rearranging the furnishings in my apartment in St. Thomas's Tower," she explained to the armourer "and would like a couple of shields to display on the wall. May I take these?"

The armourer was all too ready to please a charming lady of rank like the Duchess.

"Of course you may," he responded. "You've made a good choice there. One of these escutcheons displays the arms of the Percies, the Earls of Northumberland, and the other carries the

Neville's family coat of arms. Neville is Earl of Warwick's family name."

Lady Alice knew this full well but continued to listen attentively to the armourer who was keen to show off his knowledge of heraldry to the Duchess.

"The Percy coat of arms is very simply quartered with just the emblems of the Redvers and Warenne families. However, the Warwick shield is particularly interesting. It bears as many as seven quaterings from the various families with close family connections to the Nevilles, and includes the emblems of the Beauchamps, the Despensers, the Montacutes and the de Clares."

Lady Alice left the armoury in a state of some satisfaction. She'd realised her objectives for the morning's 'shopping' spree, and yes, both these shields are very colourful and will make wonderful wall decorations for my apartment, once they've been used for the immediately intended purpose.

Chapter 15

The Rescue

Late Thursday evening found the Lollards paddling up the Thames from Wapping where they had managed to hire the required boat. The outline of the Tower loomed through the dusk as they approached the water gate. As Constance had arranged, the gate was open and they paddled through. Constance was waiting to meet them on the other side. They moored the boat and Constance shut the gate. She then led them up the stairs which led to the living quarters of St. Thomas's Tower and knocked at the door. A voice from inside bade them enter and they came into a fairly large room, comfortably furnished with padded chairs and a bed in the corner. The walls were draped with banners bearing heraldic designs. The floor was carpeted with a large rug. This was Alice Chaucer, Duchess of Suffolk's room. She was seated on a large chair near the window across which a richly decorated curtain had been drawn. The room was adequately lit with arrays of candles. Alice looked very regal and the Lollards felt constrained to acknowledge her with a slight bow. She gestured them to sit down.

"So these are the brave men who will rescue the King," she beamed. "I feel that it was God's providence that your errand to Constance brought you here at the very moment that we became aware of the villainy afoot. This augurs well for the success of the task for which you've volunteered. The Queen is sleeping at present. She doesn't know what is planned. I haven't confided this to her for fear of heaping yet another disappointment on her should things not turn out as planned, after all the disappointment she's already experienced since her defeat at Tewkesbury. However, hopefully you will return here later tonight and then I'll wake her so that she can share just a short time with the King."

In view of the enormity of the task ahead, the Lollards had spent much of the day in prayer. This had had the effect of inducing a sense of calm upon them. However, they requested that they should spend a short time in further prayer before making their way across to the Wakefield Tower.

"Of course," said the Duchess. "We must never forget our dependency on God when embarking on a great task."

At the end of the prayers, they all took a deep breath. Constance left the room and returned with two large well-sharpened kitchen knives. The Lollards concealed these in pockets in their habits.

"I think it would be advisable for you to go with these," said the Duchess as she recovered a pair of small shields she had placed on a stool near her chair.

The Lollards then went out into the night. The air was chill. The castle precinct lights, although faint and well-spaced, were sufficient for them to find their way across to the Wakefield Tower. They cautiously entered. The door to the custodian's room was open and they correctly assumed the room was empty. They cautiously climbed the spiral stairs. The door to the King's cell opened from a small landing which punctuated the staircase. A key was in the door which they unlocked and warily entered. The room was faintly illuminated by candlelight. The

King was not in bed but kneeling at a prayer desk. He looked round in startled surprise.

"Have no fear," started Michael. "We're your friends. We've received news that someone is coming tonight to do you harm but we're here to see that this won't happen."

The King rose from his knees and gestured to them to sit on a bench in the sparsely furnished cell. He sat opposite them on a finely carved oak chair.

The Lollards brought the King up to date with a brief explanation of the situation, restricting what they said to no more than 'need to know' information. A smile of genuine joy crossed the King's face when they told him that subject to everything working out as planned, he would be able to pay a brief visit to Queen Margaret but haste was of the essence. They would have to leave her and the Tower before daybreak.

They continued their conversation quietly, keeping an attentive ear for any sound of the Tower being entered. The King bemoaned the fact that his reign had been so unsuccessful and that he hadn't been able to give Margaret the comfort and security he had wished she would enjoy as his consort.

"I wish I'd been born a shepherd rather than a king," he confided. "Many the times I've considered taking vows and entering a monastery but if God had arranged for me to be king, I knew it would be wrong to run from his purposes. Indeed, I take comfort that in my reign, I have at least been able to put into place some important things which God will be able to use in his service."

They then heard the sound they had been awaiting. Someone was ascending the stairs. They knew that this was Black Giles. The Lollards took up position between the King and the door, shields and knives at the ready. Black Giles must have been surprised to find that although there was a key in the lock, the door was not locked. He pushed open the door.

"What have we here?" he angrily declared in surprise as he saw the Lollards standing there.

"We're the King's bodyguard," answered Michael. "We will not allow you near the King. We strongly suggest that you return the way you came."

With an oath, Black Giles sprang forward, holding aloft a knife which he brought down on Michael but Michael deftly parried this with the shield supplied by the Duchess and struck upwards with his own knife. Michael was certainly not an experienced fighter but luck was on his side. The knife penetrated deeply into Black Giles' head from just below his chin. Black Giles fell backwards, striking his head heavily on a corner of the architrave round the door, fracturing his skull. Blood gushed out. He lay still. He was dead.

Next came a very messy job. They undressed the bleeding cadaver while the king disrobed from his own clothes. He dressed himself in Black Giles clothes while the Lollards shaved the face and cut the hair so that he was no longer easily recognisable as Black Giles. They dressed the body in the King's clothes and draped it, face down across the prayer desk, giving the appearance that the King had been struck from behind while at prayer.

The trio now hastily made their way down the stairs, out into the deserted castle precinct and across to St. Thomas's Tower. Constance had been standing anxiously in wait. She was shivering and glad to see the Lollards and the King emerge unscathed from the Wakefield Tower. They climbed back into the safety of St. Thomas's Tower. The Duchess was waiting. She bowed deeply before the King. They then looked at each other and laughed out loud as they suddenly felt relieved from tension. They were a terrible sight in their blood-stained clothing. The Duchess, resourceful as ever, had anticipated this and provided clean clothes for them to change into. She went to wake the Queen with the news that her husband was safe and waiting to see her. After a while, she returned. By then, the three had changed and were looking respectable. All three were provided with the sort of clothes worn by the workmen who lived in the city. The Lollards packed their bloodstained habits into the bags they always carried with them. They would be washed at the earliest opportunity. The Duchess said that she would arrange for Constance to burn

Black Giles clothing when it was safe to do so without arousing suspicion.

The King then went into Margaret's room where they were allowed time alone together. They both wept with joy to see each other again. As they talked, they were initially full of self-recrimination.

"I haven't been the king you deserved," confessed Henry. "You should have been married to a proud potentate whom none could withstand in battle. Instead, I've been a weak ineffective king."

"No, no," replied Margaret, "I alone know the wonderful things you have done as a man of peace to benefit your people. You're unique among the men who frequent the courts where I've lived, both in this country and in France. Most are proud nobles, seeking only their self- advancement with no thought for the suffering they might cause as they pursue their ambitions. You alone have been gentle and courteous and I've loved you for this. It is I who have failed you. If I'd not behaved like a proud, imperious queen towards the Duke of York, the wars we've endured may never have taken place. There's one thing I regret above all other. At the end of the second battle of St. Albans, I went against what was clearly your will. I allowed the execution of Baron Bonville and Sir Thomas Kyriell, the two Yorkist knights who had kept you from harm during the battle while you were held prisoner by the Yorkists. At the time, I was exhilarated by the victory we had won. My blood was up. I had seen so many of our brave Lancastrian knights slain before my eyes. I was in no mood to offer mercy. The crime I committed that day has haunted me ever since. My chaplain has told me that God has Bonville and Kyriell safely in his heavenly kingdom and even the sin I committed in allowing their execution can be forgiven if I am contrite and sincerely confess it. I have done so many times but still the guilt haunts me."

"Your chaplain is right," comforted Henry. "Don't think I have any regrets in having you as my queen. No king could have had a more beautiful wife, or one prepared to so resolutely defend the interests of her husband."

"What of us now?" asked Margaret. "After the death of Prince Edward at Tewkesbury, I have nothing special to live for. I hope to end my days in peaceful obscurity."

"I feel exactly the same," said Henry. "I am soon to leave this cursed castle with the Lollards who rescued me but I haven't had a chance to properly consider my future. One thing is certain however. I won't be making any attempt to recover my crown!"

The conversation between Henry and Margaret then moved to more pleasant topics, as they remembered successes and things they'd enjoyed together during the many years they shared when the country was not at war with itself. What joy Prince Edward had given them as he grew into manhood. They spoke of the pleasure they had taken on occasions when they'd crossed the river from Windsor to see the boys at play in Eton and had spoken to the teachers there. They remembered the pride with which they'd met with the students who had graduated from the colleges they had founded at Cambridge University, King's College and Queens' College. They would never see the wonderful chapel of King's College completed but already, they knew what a wonderful edifice this was going to be, something which might come to be regarded as a jewel in their crowns.

Their conversation was interrupted by the Duchess knocking at the door. She informed them that the King must leave before the imminent breaking of dawn. They clung to each other for as long as it was prudent to extend this final embrace in view of the haste needed for the King to leave the Tower safely.

Henry re-entered the Duchess' room. He warmly thanked Alice Chaucer for her invaluable service, not just to Margaret but in being key to the success of this escape. The Lollards and the King, accompanied by Constance, made their way down to their boat moored by the water gate which later ages have dubbed 'Traitor's Gate'. They settled in their boats, the Lollards and the King in the boat hired from Wapping and Constance in the smaller boat which she would need to access the gate and open it. Then they froze at the sound of armoured feet making their way from the Byward Tower. This was the Tower guard moving round the castle to relieve the sentries on duty. They huddled down as deeply as they could in their boats. Their alarm was short lived. In the darkness, the guard never suspected nor noticed that there were occupants in the boats. They breathed again as the armoured footsteps receded as the guard approached Tower Green where the sentry outside the Constable's house would be changed. Constance quietly paddled out to the gate and opened it so that the Lollards and King could pass through. They waved a farewell to her as they steered their boat to to the River Thames beyond. Constance closed the gate behind them and returned to St. Thomas's Tower. The plan had been successfully accomplished but now she relieved the tension she had been under by bursting into floods of tears as she settled back into her room. Lady Alice shared Constance's relief that everything had gone as well as could have been hoped for and settled down to sleep for the few hours remaining before day would fully break.

Dawn was just beginning to break as the Lollards paddled back to Wapping where they disembarked. They moored the boat at the point from which they had hired it the day before. They then went to the lodging which the Lollards had rented the previous day. They knew that they couldn't take the King to the house of just anyone who had been prepared to offer two missionaries hospitality but Constance had given them more than enough money to hire the boat. They used some of the money left over to secure this lodging. On entering their room, all three of them fell on to the beds and in no time were sound asleep, at last able to fully relax. after the tension of the previous night.

The following morning, the custodian of the Wakefield Tower returned to his duty and found as he had expected what he believed to be the murdered king lying across his prayer desk. He immediately went to inform the Constable of the Tower, John Sutton, Baron Dudley, who sent two servants with a coffin in which the murdered king was to be placed. They had no real idea of what the king looked like and it was probably an unnecessary precaution to disguise the identity of the body by shaving and cutting the hair of Black Giles. The servants didn't even query in their minds the fact that the knife by the body was completely clean with no bloody residue. Baron Dudley reported that the king had died in the night and steps were taken to have him interred with due ceremony in Chertsey Abbey.

Meanwhile, the Lollards had to plan for the future of King Henry. There was no chance he could again contest the crown and this was the last thing he wanted to do. Knowing that during their conversation in the Wakefield Tower, Henry (we will no longer call him King) had spoken of the many times he had considered taking holy orders and becoming a monk, they explored with him the possibility of entering a monastery and doing just that. Henry was readily agreeable to this suggestion and he further indicated that Waverley Abbey in Surrey would be the place he would like to spend his last days. Waverley was prestigious in that it was the mother house of the Cistercian order in England.

They set out at a leisurely pace for Waverley and reached it after three days. Henry was so grateful for the enlightening conversation that he had had with Matthew and Michael as they made their journey to Waverley. He acknowledged that he was learning spiritual truths from the Lollards which he had previously only vaguely understood. They in turn were impressed to see that in spite of the tumult of the previous evening's rescue, Henry had taken with him from his cell, as one of his most treasured possessions, a well-read copy of John Wycliffe's Bible in English.

The Abbott of Waverley, William Martyn, was surprised by the arrival of two Lollards accompanied by a would-be postulant. Henry was introduced as brother Hal although there was no need to disguise the fact that he was usually known as Henry. There was no way that the Abbott could possibly recognise him as the former King Henry.

The Abbott interviewed them very carefully to make sure this wasn't a casual approach. Although the Lollards weren't applying to enter the Abbey themselves, the Abbott was nonetheless very interested in the way they lived out their lives and thoroughly approved of their discipline. He didn't feel unduly constrained by edicts from the pope and was aware of, and somewhat in agreement with, the teachings of John Wycliffe.

Obviously, he specially focused his interrogation on Henry, the would-be postulant. Henry had to explain what it was in his background that caused him to consider taking this step. Henry had to be very careful in answering this question. He merely said that he was disillusioned through the situations in which the wars had placed him where he had felt pressure to do things which he felt to be morally wrong. These pressures would not exist in an establishment whose prime concern was to serve God. The Abbott appreciated and accepted this answer without probing further. He was impressed by the evidence which indicated that Henry was highly educated and was well acquainted with the contents of the Bible. Abbott William Martyn had no problem in admitting Henry as a postulant.

The Lollards stayed overnight in the Abbey and in the morning, said their farewell to Henry as they prepared to leave. Henry was an emotional man whose feelings were always just below the surface and difficult to disguise. He wept with gratitude as he hugged the Lollards goodbye. A new life was going to open before him where he would no longer have to bear the burdens of being the king of an unruly country.

Chapter 16

Rewards and Punishments

A great maxim of the Christian life is that we should forgive our enemies. If we find that exercising this forgiveness is very difficult, at least we need to curb any desire to take revenge ourselves on those who have wronged us for the Bible teaches in both the Old and New Testaments that it is God's prerogative to carry out any vengeance needed

> ***"Vengeance is mine. I will repay," says the Lord.***
> ***Deuteronomy ch 32 v 35, Romans ch 12 v 19***

All of us have experienced wrongs, perhaps severe wrongs, in our lives. If we desist in the desire for personal revenge, how often do we find that the one who has wronged us experiences a serious setback themselves. Can we regard this as God extracting vengeance on our behalf without there being any need for us to take retributive action ourselves? Should we persist in seeking revenge, we would be seriously failing to conform to Biblical teaching. Even if we don't witness what we might regard as divine retribution in this life, we may be sure that it will be meted out in the next. God is perfectly just and able to judge wrongs far more reliably than can we fallible humans. Many wrong deeds have been recounted in the story you have just read. If we follow through by studying what happened in subsequent history, we may see many examples of how these wrong doers were recompensed in what we may regard as divine justice operating in this life. In the same way, those who do good are often rewarded in this life without having to wait for 'the well done thou good and faithful servant' in the next.

A year or so after Henry's rescue, Margaret was ransomed by King Louis XI and returned to France where she resided in a castle near her birthplace at Dampier-sur-Loire in Anjou. This is not so far from L'Aumbone Abbey in Normandy, the mother house of Waverley Abbey where Henry was serving as a monk under the name of Brother Hal. We may only speculate on whether Margaret got to know that Henry was now a monk in the prime Cistercian Abbey in England and could keep in contact with him through the communications which took place across the network of European Cistercian abbeys.

Constance, her lady-in-waiting, was willing to accompany Margaret back to France but Margaret considered this would be unfair to Constance whose roots were in England.

"In any case," said Margaret, "I have only borrowed you from Lady de Ros. You have given me such wonderful service but I mustn't selfishly keep what really belongs to another. I have been so blessed by having you with me through this very difficult time but Lady de Ros who's lost her husband serving the Lancastrian cause, has first call on your services."

Margaret spent her remaining seven years living peacefully in Anjou. On her death, she was buried near her parents in Angers Cathedral.

So it was that Constance returned to Helmsley where she enjoyed a joyful reunion with Philippa de Ros and with Matthew and Michael. It was wonderful to see Edmund, now grown into manhood, filling his father's shoes as the new Baron de Ros and responsibly running the castle and its associated estates. The orphanage Matthew and Michael had founded was now completely built and furnished and was functioning as well as the Lollards could have possibly hoped in caring for and educating the local orphans.

Michael had noticed how well Matthew and Constance hit it off and realised how strongly they were attracted to each other. He was correct in his belief that they had fallen in love

"Why don't you ask her to marry you?" he challenged Michael.

"Agreeable as the prospect of marrying Constance would be," Michael sadly replied, "I can't really ask a woman to share the sort of life we lead, often sleeping rough, having no money to call our own. It just wouldn't be fair to Constance, even if she'd have me."

Matthew and Michael were now finding that the rough living associated with their frequent excursions to carry out missionary work was beginning to take a toll on their health. This was something that the Vicar, Will Hakford, had noticed and he invited them to the vicarage where he made a suggestion which totally surprised them. He told them that George Neville, the Archbishop of York and brother of the former Earl of Warwick, had died and was being replaced by Lawrence Booth who had been a Lancastrian supporter.

"I never really hit it off with George Neville but Lawrence is a very different sort of man," Will told the Lollards, "Lawrence hasn't consistently supported the Lancastrian cause but throughout this wretched war, so many people have changed sides and back again more than once so I won't hold this against him. He's made a point of meeting all the incumbents in the diocese which has given me a chance to get to know him as a person. I am impressed with the new Archbishop. He's a wise and fair-minded man. One of the things he was urging incumbents of the churches' for which he had spiritual oversight' to do was to identify men who would be suitable for the ministry. You both came immediately to mind. Indeed, you're already ministers in the true sense of the word in a way that I know many of my fellow clergy aren't. I know you don't hold with so much of what goes on in the church, its wealth and show, but bear in mind that the founder of your movement was a member of the clergy. Indeed, John Wycliffe was Vicar of Lutterworth until his death. I obviously don't expect an answer from you immediately so go away and think about what I've said. If you do decide to enter the ministry and the Archbishop is agreeable, you'd be able to serve your curacies in my parish until vacancies come up elsewhere for you to take over as parish priests."

Matthew and Michael went away to think this over and it didn't take them long to come to a conclusion. Now that it was clear that their missionary days were coming to an end, this made perfect sense as a way in which they could continue to serve God.

Two days later, they returned to Will Hakford who was delighted with their response.

"I'll arrange for you to see the Archbishop at his earliest convenience," he told them. "I have no doubt that he'll welcome you with open arms but be circumspect in what you say. No Pope bashing and when the matter of Holy Communion comes up, explain the doctrine of consubstantiation as carefully as you did to me."

Needless to say, the Lollards were accepted as admirable candidates for the ministry. Matthew now felt that he could ask Constance to marry him and she accepted his proposal. They were married by Will Hakford at All Saints, Helmsley parish church, amid great rejoicing from all who had come to know and love them as individuals.

It wasn't long before Matthew and Michael were both vicars of parishes within York diocese. Michael was married himself a short time later.

What of other characters involved in this narrative. King Edward fell out with his brother, the unfaithful George, Duke of Clarence, and Clarence was consigned to the Tower. Only those who lived within the Tower knew what happened to George but they all observed the code of secrecy observed by those who resided and worked within this grim castle. Legend has it that he was drowned by his gaolers in a butt of malmsey but this is probably just fanciful folklore.

Anne, the Earl of Warwick's daughter, was widowed when Henry and Margaret's son was killed at the Battle of Tewkesbury. This freed her to marry the love of her life, Richard, Duke of Gloucester. Anne thus became Queen but as the bride of Richard rather than the wife of the son of Henry and Margaret as her father had planned. In some ways, Anne and her son may be considered fortunate to have died of natural causes a year before King Richard was killed at the Battle of Bosworth.

What of the de Ros's arch enemy, Baron John Howard. He never knew why Black Giles didn't return to collect his reward but assumed that he had been taken into the King's service to perform other dark deeds. At first, John Howard seemed to be riding the wave of good fortune. He was a favourite of the new king, Edward IV who awarded John the duchy of Norfolk and the title, Earl Marshall of England. Edward died prematurely and unexpectedly and his young son, Edward, aged twelve become the nominal king as Edward V. Edward's uncle, Richard, Duke of Gloucester, had been nominated by the former king, his brother, to be Protector of England. He arranged for the new king to stay in the Tower of London for his 'safety'. John Howard, now a Duke, persuaded the former Queen, Elizabeth

Woodville, to allow her other young son, Richard, Duke of York, to join the Prince of Wales in the Tower so that he would have company. Elizabeth agreed but against her better judgement. She had taken sanctuary in Westminster Abbey because she distrusted Richard of Gloucester. The young boys were never seen again outside the Tower. Yet another unexplained assassination within this grim fortress. Though it is commonly suspected that their murder had been arranged by Richard, Duke of Gloucester, so that he could ascend to the throne as King Richard III, there is no conclusive evidence that he was responsible and the jury is out concerning the young princes' fate. John Howard, Duke of Norfolk, one of King Richard's right hand men was killed with his master on Bosworth Field.

It is worth mentioning a unique document which must be of great interest to historians. This document is called 'Titulus Regius' and was prepared and submitted to Parliament by Richard III to substantiate his right to the throne. The document provided evidence that King Edward IV's marriage to Elizabeth Woodville was bigamous, thus making his children, Edward, Richard and Elizabeth illegitimate. Parliament accepted the validity of this document and enacted it as a law. Thus, there would have been no actual reason for Richard to murder his nephews as they were now officially illegitimate.

With the death of Richard on the battlefield, the throne passed to the remaining Lancastrian heir, Henry Tudor, Earl of Richmond, whose faint claim to the throne came through his mother, Margaret Beaufort, great great granddaughter of John of Gaunt, Duke of Lancaster. For Henry VII, 'Titulus Regius' was a very inconvenient document for not only did it contradict Henry's contention that he was right in removing Richard III as a usurper but pronounced his intended wife, Elizabeth, as illegitimate along with her brothers. The new king therefore got Parliament to repeal the Act and ordered all copies of this sensitive document to be destroyed without being first read. Thus, Edward IVs son was confirmed to have been the rightful King Edward V during his short life and Henry VII's grandson succeeded to the throne as Edward VI. Further, his new wife, Elizabeth, was now regarded as the fully legitimate daughter of the previous king, Edward IV. The marriage of Henry and Elizabeth thus united the warring houses of York and Lancaster and further attempts to revive the Lancastrian cause were easily defeated. Only one copy of Titulus Regius survived and this wasn't discovered until James I's reign, one hundred years later, that is, after the Tudor dynasty had died out.

Having been a staunch opponent of the House of York, John Howard was posthumously attainted by the new king, Henry VII. This meant that his title, Duke of Norfolk, didn't automatically pass to his son, Thomas. However, Thomas, Earl of Surrey, earned this title back by virtue of his leading the army which defeated the invading Scots at the Battle of Flodden in the reign of Henry VIII. Notable among John Howard's descendants were his great granddaughters, Anne Boleyn and Catherine Howard, both wives of King Henry VIII, who were executed on the grounds of their infidelity.

What does posterity have to say of King Henry VI and his Queen, Margaret? They probably go down as failed kings and queens of England, but that appraisal doesn't take account of their lasting legacy to the country. How many of our great laws and institutions can be directly attributed to earlier kings? King John can hardly take credit for Magna Carta, nor can King Henry III take any credit for the Parliament which had been set up by Simon de Montfort. On the other hand, King Henry and Queen Margaret made a lasting contribution to the education of the nation when they founded Eton College and the two colleges, King's and Queens', in Cambridge University. Over one third of the Prime Ministers of the United Kingdom were educated at Eton. A list of these Prime Ministers is included as an appendix to this book. A list has also been included in the appendix of just some of the eminent men who were educated at King's College. Had she lived in another age, Queen Margaret would have strongly championed the cause of female education. Although when they founded these colleges, entry to universities was restricted to men, women are now admitted to university on the same basis as men. Thus, in another appendix, a list of some of the eminent women who attended Queens' college is provided. Yes, Henry and Margaret left to the nation a valuable legacy which lasts to this day and which will continue. Queen Margaret has the further distinction of being the only person who features in four of Shakespeare's plays.

Whatever his shortcomings, no one disputes the fact that Henry VI was a very saintly man. Henry Tudor applied to the Vatican to have him canonised. Everything seemed to be going well with this application until the negotiations which needed to be concluded for this to happen faltered when England split with the Pope in the reign of Henry VIII. Thus Henry was never officially recognised as Saint Henry. It was arranged that Henry's remains should be transferred from Chertsey Abbey to his birthplace and they now reside in St. George's Chapel, Windsor. Although we know the actual identity of the body believed to be that of Henry of Windsor, only those who have read this book will be aware of the deception. How then did many who visited Henry's shrine experience miraculous cures on touching his grave? Many others had claimed similar miracles had taken place when they touched a piece of what they were told was a relic from the true cross. We know that so many pieces of wood described as relics of the true cross were circulating in Europe at the time that very few if any could be genuine. We can only conclude that miraculous cures have more to do with the faith of the person who experiences the miracle than the authenticity or power of the relic being touched to effect the miracle. Such was the reputation of Henry of Windsor that his grave became the focus of pilgrimages of those who hoped and expected to see great wonders take place.

A further legacy of King Henry to the nation is something which is both visible and audible in this modern day. Although not completed until after his lifetime, the chapel of King's College which he endowed and whose design he approved, is one of the most beautiful buildings in England. Gothic architecture reached its zenith in the perpendicular style of which King's College Chapel is a prime example, so light and airy with its large delicate widows and elaborate fan vaulting. One of the delights enjoyed at Christmas by so many, even living beyond England's shores, is the annual service of twelve lessons and carols broadcast annually from King's College Chapel.

Line of descent of House of Lancaster

Edward III = Philippa (daughter of William,
1327 - 1377 Count of Hainault and Holland)
d. 1369

John of Gaunt = Blanche (daughter of Henry,
Duke of Lancaster Duke of Lancaster)
d. 1399

Henry IV = Mary (daughter of Humphrey de
1399-1413 Bohun, Earl of Hereford & Essex)
d. 1394

Henry V = Catherine (daughter of Charles VI,
1413-1422 King of France)
d. 1437

Henry VI = Margaret (daughter of Rene,
1422-1461 Duke of Anjou)
1470-1471 d. 1482

Edward, Prince of Wales = Anne (daughter of Richard
killed at Battle of Neville Earl of Warwick)
Tewkesbury 1471 d. 1485

Line of descent of House of York

Edward III = Philippa (daughter of William,
1327 - 1377 Count of Hainault and Holland)

Lionel of Antwerp = Elizabeth, (daughter of William de
Duke of Clarence Burgh Earl of Ulster)
d. 1368

Philippa = Edmund Mortimer
Countess of Ulster Earl of March d 1381

Roger Mortimer = Eleanor (dau of Thomas Holland
Earl of March Earl of Kent)
killed 1398 d. 1405

Anne Mortimer = Richard, Earl of Cambridge
 beheaded 1415

Richard, **Duke of York** = Cecily (dau of Ralph Neville
killed at Battle of Earl of Westmorland)
Wakefield 1460

Edward IV = Elizabeth (daughter of   **Richard III** = Anne
1461 – 1483 | Richard Woodville   1483-85   (dau of
 Earl Rivers)   Earl of Warwick)
           d 1485

Edward V 1483   Edward
murdered 1483   Prince of Wales d 1484

Battles fought during the Hundred Years War

Year	Battle	Victor	Significant Outcome
1337	Cadzand	England	
1338	Amemuiden	France	
1340	Sluys	England	Franco-Genoese fleet destroyed ensuring England will not be invaded.
1340	St. Omer	France	Strategic withdrawal of Anglo-Flemish forces
1340	Tournai	France	Siege of Tournai relieved
1341	Champtoceaux	France	
1342	Brest	England	
1342	Mortaix	France	
1345	Auberoche	England	
1346	St. Pol de Leon	England	
1346	Caen	England	Caen was sacked
1346	Blanchetaque	England	English able to ford river
1346	**Crecy**	England	English archers soundly defeated French cavalry
1346	Neville's Cross	England	
1346-7	Siege of Calais	England	
1347	La Roche-Derrien	England	
1350	Les Espagnoles Sur Mer	England	English fleet defeats Castilian fleet in close fight
1351	St. Jean dAngely	France	

Battles fought during the Hundred Years War

Year	Battle	Victor	Significant Outcome
1351	Ardres	France	
1351	Thirty	France	0 French knights versus 30 English knights
1352	Mauron	England	
1353	Lsignan	France	
1353	Comborn	England	
1354	Montmuran	France	
1356	**Poitiers**	England	The Black Prince captures King John II – France plunged into chaos
1364	Cocherel	France	
1364	Auray	England	French general du Guesclin captured
1367	Najera	England	
1369	Montiel	France	
1370	Limoges	England	
1370	Pontvallain	France	
1372	La Rochelle	Castille	French Castilian allies defeat English fleet, depriving England of naval supremacy
1373	Chisel	France	
1382	Roosebeke	France	
1383	Ypres	French	

Battles fought during the Hundred Years War

Year	Battle	Victor	Significant Outcome
1385	Invasion of Scotland	England	French army landed in Scotland forced to retreat
1385	Allubarrota	Portugal	Franco-Castilian forces defeated by Portuguese supported by English archers
1387	Margate	England	Franco-Castilian fleet defeated, ending French invasion threat
1404	Blackpool Sands	England	
1415	Harfleur	England	
1415	**Agincourt**	England	Small English army defeats much larger French army Henry V becomes heir to French throne.
1418	Rouen	England	
1419	La Rochelle	Castille	Castilian fleet defeats English fleet
1420	Fresnay	Engamd	Defeat of large Franco-Scottish army
1421	Bauge	France	Franco-Scottish army Defeats English
1422	Meaux	England	Henry V falls ill at siege and dies aged 35
1423	Cravant	England	Franco-Scottish army defeated
1423	Brossiniere	France	

Battles fought during the Hundred Years War

Year	Battle	Victor	Significant Outcome
1424	Verneuil	England	Decisive defeat of Franco-Scottish army
1426	St. James	England	French besieging army dispersed by small English force
1428	**Orleans**	France	Siege relieved by French army with Joan of Arc
1429	Herrings	England	
1429	Jargeau	France	
1429	Meung-sur-Loire	France	French capture district along Loire
1429	Beaugency	France	
1429	**Patay**	France	Joan of Arc destroys English rearguard of archers and defeats English army
1435	Gerbergy	France	
1449	Rouen	France	City regained from English
1450	Formigny	France	Heavy English casualties
1453	**Castillon**	France	French use of cannon was major factor in determining French victory

End of Hundred Years War.

Battles fought during the War of the Roses

Date	Battle	Victors	Significant Outcome
22/05/**1455**	1st St. Alban's	Yorkists	
23/09/**1459**	Blore Heath	Yorkists	
12/10/**1459**	Ludford Bridge	Lancastrians	Richard, Duke of York, fled to Ireland
10/07/**1460**	Northampton	Yorkists	Henry VI captured, Margaret fled to Wales
13/12/**1460**	Wakefield	Lancastrians	Richard, Duke of York, killed
02/02/**1461**	Mortimer's Cross	Yorkists	
17/02/**1461**	2nd St. Albans	Lancastrians	Henry VI rescued
28/03/**1461**	Ferrybridge	Yorkist	Edward of York proclaimed King Edward IV
29/03/**1461**	Towton	Yorkists	Henry VI and Margaret fled to Scotland
25/04/**1464**	Hedgeley Moor	Yorkists	Henry VI captured and imprisoned in Tower of London

Battles fought during the War of the Roses

Date	Battle	Victors	Significant Outcome
15/05/**1464**	Hexham	Yorkists	Baron Thomas de Ros executed
	Earl of Warwick changes sides and restores Henry VI to the throne		
26/07/**1469**	Edgecote Moor	Lancastrians	Edward IV imprisoned at Middleham
12/03/**1470**	Losecote Field	Yorkists	
14/04/**1471**	Barnet	Yorkists	Earl of Warwick killed
04/05/**1471**	Tewkesbury	Yorkists	Henry VI and Queen Margaret captured. Prince of Wales killed. Edward IV undisputed King
22/08/**1485**	Bosworth	Lancastrians/ Tudors	Richard III killed. Henry Tudor becomes King. Henry VII
16/06/**1487**	Stoke Field	Tudors	Earl of Lincoln Killed. Lambert Simnel captured

List of Old Etonian Prime Ministers

Robert Walpole		1721-1742
John Stuart	Earl of Bute	1762-1763
William Pitt the Elder	Earl of Chatham	1766-1768
Frederick North	Earl of Guildford	1770-1782
William Grenville		1806-1807
George Canning		1827
Arthur Wellesley	Duke of Wellington	1828-1830, 1834
Charles Grey	Earl Grey	1830-1834
William Lamb	Viscount Melbourne	1834, 1835-1841
Edward Smith Stanley	Earl of Derby	1852, 1858-1859, 1866-1868
William Gladstone		1868-1874, 1880-1885, 1886, 1892-1894
Robert Cecil	Marquess of Salisbury	1885-1886, 1886-1892, 1895-1902
Archibald Primrose	Earl of Rosebury	1894-1895
Arthur Balfour	Earl of Balfour	1902-1905
Anthony Eden	Earl of Avon	1955-1957
Harold Macmillan	Earl of Stckton	1957-1963
Alec Douglas-Home	Baron Home	1963-1964
David Cameron		2010-2017
Boris Johnson		2020

A few of the Prominent Alumni of King's College, Cambridge University

Rupert Brooke	Poet
Alan Turing	Computer Scientist & Cryptologist
E. M. Forster	Novelist
John Maynard Keynes	Economist
Salman Rushdie	Novelist
Patrick Blackett	Physicist, Nobel Laureate
Marin Bell	Politician
Richard Cox	Bishop of Ely
Karl Pearson	Mathematician
Mervyn King	Governor of the Bank of England
Zadie Smith	Novelist
Orlando Gibbons	Composer
Francis Walsingham	Elizabethan Spymaster
Robert Walpole	Prime Minister
Tom Dalyell	Politician
John Bird	Comedian
Colin Redgrave	Actor
Sir David Willcocks	Choral Conductor
High Dalton	Chancellor of the Exchequer

A few of the Prominent Female Alumni and Fellows of Queens' College, Cambridge University

Liz Kendall	Candidate for Leadership of Labour Party
Elizabeth Day	Journalist and Novelist
Emily Maitlis	Journalist, Documentary Maker & News Reader
Hannah Murray	Actress
June Osborne	Chair of UK Bioindustry Association
Dr. Pippa Wells	Physicist
Lydia Wilson	Actress
Dr. Ella McPherson	Sociologist
Prof. Marie Edwards	Volcanologist
Suella Braverman	Attorney General
Stephanie Merritt	Novelist

The books published by Midhurst have been written by Dr Ray Filby who has had many years' experience of church life in a number of churches, fulfilling at various times the roles of Pathfinder Group Leader, Youth Fellowship Leader, Secretary to the Parochial Church Council, Churchwarden and Reader (Licensed Lay Minister). This experience is reflected in the stories he writes which embrace several genres, including historical fiction, short stories, Bible study, murder stories, romantic fiction and science fiction. They are all available from Amazon in paperback or Kindle form.

The Sun and the Moon of Alexandria

This is a fictional biopic of Apollos, a missionary saint and one of St. Paul's co-workers. Although mentioned many times in the New Testament, little is known of the life and background of Apollos. Thus, there is scope to create a story which constructs a feasible account of Apollos' youth in Egypt, his journey to Israel, his conversion, his relationship with St. Paul, his missionary work and his marriage. The story culminates in his martyrdom. In situations where Apollos interacts with well-known Biblical characters, the narrative remains faithful to the New Testament account.
(This book is published by the Book Guild)

Parables, the Greatest Stories ever told - Retold

'The Greatest Stories ever told – Retold' focuses on the better known parables of Jesus and rewrites them as situations in modern life which correspond to the situations in Jesus' day, attempting to promote the same teaching that Jesus was giving in the original parable. Each parable is preceded by a modern translation of the original parable and followed by ten questions which are suitable for a person's private devotions or for use in the context of a group Bible study.

St. Columba's – Its Life and Its People

Churches are living organisms, each with their own distinctive patterns of life. While their members experience the same ups and downs in life as the population as a whole, their Christian faith results in their reacting to circumstances in a distinctive way.

This book is a set of short stories, some of which trace the unfolding of events which occur as part of church life, and others which recount the experience of individual church members. Readers are invited to consider the practical or ethical problems which arise in these stories and think how they themselves might have dealt with or reacted to these situations.

The Countess who should have been Queen

Margaret Plantagenet was born near the end of the Wars of the Roses. As the daughter of the brother of King Edward IV, a situation could well have arisen when she or her brother, Edward, had a claim to the throne. Margaret was not ambitious to become Queen but was happy to marry a commoner and settled as an enlightened landowner with her husband in Berkshire. Margaret became Queen Catherine of Aragon's chief lady-in-waiting and was awarded a peerage to become Countess of Salisbury. Margaret faithfully supported Catherine right through her reign and as far as she could when Catherine was sent to live in isolation after her divorce. One of Margaret's sons, Reginald, became a prominent churchman and angered the King by writing a treatise, heavily critical of Henry VIII, the way he had divorced Catherine and taken over the Church of England. Reginald was living out of reach of Henry on the continent so Henry vented his wrath on Margaret and her family.

Consequences of Immature Love

Boy-Girl, Man-Woman relationships cement our society. Because these relationships are seldom straightforward, they provide scope for an indefinite number of works of fiction. In this novel, you are invited to follow the amorous adventures of Georgina Matthews and Arthur Gray from the time they leave school and start at university until they ultimately marry the partner for whom they seemed destined from the outset.

The story told might be of special interest to a young person embarking on the minefield of love and courtship as they consider the factors which led to the success or failure of the relationships encountered in this novel. Ethical factors are involved and it is significant that a shared Christian faith led to the final happy outcome.

Soldiers, Saints and Sinners

'*Soldiers, Saints and Sinners*' is a collection of fictitious stories, featuring some of the minor characters whom Jesus encountered in his ministry. It attempts to suggest how their backgrounds might have been important in the way they led to their encounter with Jesus and the way these encounters furthered the progress of Jesus' ministry. Each story is preceded by a modern Biblical translation of the passage which recounts their appearance on the scene where Jesus was ministering and is followed by five questions which are suitable for a person's private devotions or for use in the context of a group Bible study.

The Tasks of Chronavon

When sensible twelve-year-olds, Alfred and Alice meet a mysterious angel called Chronavon in the vestry of their church, it seems someone is playing a practical joke on them. After all, angels don't just pop up in church vestries to enlist the help of two young people to journey back in time to prevent a devilish time traveller from altering the course of history. Yet it soon becomes clear that Chronavon's incredible story is true. As Alfred and Alice are whisked backwards through the centuries, they become immersed in the rich customs and costumes of the past through Henry III's troubled reign, the insecurity of Princess Elizabeth before she became Queen Elizabeth I and the Civil War between the Cavaliers and Roundheads. 'The Tasks of Chronavon' is an exciting, informative tale for young readers which effortlessly weaves fact and fiction with a sprinkling of humour and shows how little human values have changed over time.

The Evil Occupants of Easingdale Castle

Teenager, Jason, and his friends, Bill, Becky and Liz, are recruited by an unusual messenger to pit their wits against an international gang of forgers, occupying their local castle. The gang are intent on destabilising the British economy by flooding the country with forged £20 notes which could pass off as the real thing. The gang is well equipped with hi-tech machines.

It remains to be seen whether Jason and his friends, who are also technically knowledgeable, can outwit the gang.

Technology will have advanced since this book was written and young readers are invited to consider whether they could have done better than Jason and his friends with equipment now available.

A Church like Cluedo

After graduating from college as a civil engineer, Annette Owen had hoped to work in the developing world under the auspices of a missionary society. When this door to Christian service was closed, she applied to become an ordained minister but was turned down by the selection committee. She was however able to exercise a very fulfilled ministry as a clergy wife. Unfortunately, her clergy husband had dark secrets in his life of which Annette was totally unaware until a situation arose which resulted in murder being committed. The impact of this had an unexpected effect on the course of Annette's life.

Inspector Sinclair and Sergeant Powers' most interesting cases

This account of some interesting cases solved by the detective duo, Inspector Sinclair and Sergeant Powers, is not a normal 'whodunnit' in which the murderer is not revealed until the very end when the detective reveals the clues which he or she alone has picked up to solve the case without sharing their significance with the reader until the very end.

The stories in this book are divided into sections, a list of those involved to help the reader keep track of the characters,

'the Event' which describes the situation when the murder took place,

'the Investigation' which describes the systematic way in which the detectives investigated the case and

'the Evidence' in which the crucial evidence by which a cast iron case against the murderer was built up, is reviewed.

An Insight into the Gospels and the Book of Acts

'An Insight into the Gospels and the Book of Acts' is an overview of the themes, contents, emphases, and structure of the first five books of the New Testament. While there is so much similarity in the stories and teaching in each of the gospels, this book contrasts the way each gospel is written and presented. It highlights the quite remarkable differences which exist between each of the gospels as they are directed to different audiences and have different primary objectives. The book is presented with the main content of the book appearing on the right hand (odd numbered) pages and supportive texts placed opposite the relevant passages on the left hand pages.

Puzzles, Quiz and Activities Suitable for Social Events
Volumes 1, 2, 3, 4, 5 & 6

These books consist of a set of puzzles, quiz and activities which the author designed for use at a monthly social event organised by St. Michael's, Church, Budbrooke, in the Community Centre in the part of the parish known as Chase Meadow. People who have opted to take part really seem to have enjoyed these activities which are interesting rather than extremely challenging. While a good general knowledge is helpful in completing some of the activities, they are not designed to expose people's ignorance as data sheets and appropriate reference books like atlases are made available to help participants find any information needed. Thus, the activities are educational.

The socials run at Chase Meadow are not restricted to church members but all and sundry are invited as part of the church outreach. With many of the activities, a final stage often involves deciphering a phrase, quote or saying. As the socials are sponsored by the church, many of the quotes to be deciphered are Biblical texts. However, anyone choosing to use these ideas could quite easily modify the final stage and use a secular quote rather than a Biblical text to be deciphered.

Planets, Plagues and Pandemics

Klandacia, a planet orbiting a nearby star, has a technology well in advance of that on earth. A pandemic, similar to the coronavirus outbreak experienced on earth, has caused the death of many Klandacians and is a recent memory to the humanoid population of this planet. As the Klandacians have developed an economy which is cashless, it came out of the pandemic without the economic turmoil experienced on earth as it emerges from the coronavirus pandemic. The Klandacian Supreme High Priest receives a message from God requesting that help should be sent to earth. Although the journey to earth will take many years, four Klandacian astronauts volunteer for the mission, two men and two women. On reaching earth, the astronauts are able to acclimatise to earth's culture during a short time spent with a Moravian community, learning key languages they will need on earth. However, the Klandacians experience one serious mishap before they can return to their home planet.

www.ingramcontent.com/pod-product-compliance
Lightning Source LLC
LaVergne TN
LVHW051225070526
838200LV00057B/4602